PUFFIN

INCUBUS

Your father didn't trust me, Danny.

I scared him.

Do I scare you, Danny?

Are you as weak as your father?

Nick Gifford also writes adult novels under the name Keith Brooke. As well as writing, Nick develops websites and lives with his wife and children in north-east Essex.

www.nickgifford.co.uk

Nick has ensured that the site featured in this book, www.spirit-talking.co.uk, has been made safe for you to visit. However, please note: readers are advised not to go on spirit-talking boards or ouija sites unsupervised.

Books by Nick Gifford

FLESH AND BLOOD

INCUBUS

PIGGIES

NICK GIFFORD

INCUBUS

PUFFIN

PUFFIN BOOKS

Published by the Penguin Group
Penguin Books Ltd, 80 Strand, London WC2R 0RL, England
Penguin Group (USA), Inc., 375 Hudson Street, New York, New York 10014, USA
Penguin Books Australia Ltd, 250 Camberwell Road, Camberwell, Victoria 3124, Australia
Penguin Books Canada Ltd, 10 Alcorn Avenue, Toronto, Ontario, Canada M4V 3B2
Penguin Books India (P) Ltd, 11 Community Centre, Panchsheel Park, New Delhi – 110 017, India
Penguin Group (NZ), cnr Airborne and Rosedale Roads, Albany, Auckland 1310, New Zealand
Penguin Books (South Africa) (Pty) Ltd, 24 Sturdee Avenue, Rosebank 2196, South Africa

Penguin Books Ltd, Registered Offices: 80 Strand, London WC2R 0RL, England

www.penguin.com

First published 2005
1

Set in 11.5/15.5pt Monotype Bembo
Typeset by Rowland Phototypesetting Ltd, Bury St Edmunds, Suffolk
Made and printed in England by Clays Ltd, St Ives plc

British Library Cataloguing in Publication Data
A CIP catalogue record for this book is available from the British Library

ISBN 0-141-31731-0

The kobold text on page 93 is from www.longlongtimeago.com

For Eric, Sarah and Yvonne
Three who made all the difference

Contents

1

Like Father, Like Son

'Do you not see it, Danny? You think my eyes have gone just because I'm seventy-four and I take my teeth out every night?' Oma Schmidt cackled and rubbed at the damp corner of her mouth with the cuff of her cardigan.

Danny Smith took the photo from her and stared at it, holding it steady as the train juddered and rolled.

Each time they visited Danny's father, she had to do something like this. Find something to bring. It might be a photo or an old magazine, or once even an item of clothing, an old jumper. Something from the past, from when things had been so much better. Something to comfort her, and maybe she thought it would comfort her grandson, Danny, too.

'You tell me I'm wrong?' she demanded.

No, he saw it.

The photograph was creased, the corners curled and thickened where the layers were coming apart. The colours were faded as if they were being washed away.

A boy stared out of the picture. He sat on what was probably a brand new bicycle. A large child on a bike that was too small, but the boy was still grinning. Proud. His long, frizzy hair was cut short at the front and on top, and he wore flared trousers and a jumper with multi-coloured horizontal stripes across the front. The bike was an ugly-looking thing: small wheels with thick tyres, long handlebars sticking up and then bent down at each end, an extended saddle with a backrest thrust upwards at right angles.

He saw it all right.

It was in the eyes. Eyes that stared back at him from the bathroom mirror each morning when he washed.

The boy in the photo was about fourteen, the same age that Danny was now. Like the boy in the photo, he was tall and awkward, in a body that somehow seemed too big and angular for him. The boy in the photo, sitting proudly on his new Chopper bike, was Danny's father and, stupid 1970s haircut and clothes aside, he looked just like Danny.

'You could be twins, eh?' said Oma, nudging Danny sharply with a bony elbow. 'You are so alike.'

Danny looked away, out of the window. He stared at the graffiti on the walls and buildings they were passing. He was not like his father.

He was *not* like his father.

He still had the photo. He wanted to tear it up into little pieces and throw them out of the window, watch the shower of photograph-confetti spreading over the tracks, being left safely far behind.

He was not like his father.

He had self-control.

He looked down and saw that his knuckles were white

where he gripped the photograph. He made himself relax, and handed the snap back to his grandmother.

'They won't let you take it in,' he told her. They weren't allowed to take things into the visiting hall. 'They'll make you leave it in your bag in one of the lockers.'

She smiled and tapped the side of her head. 'I have it up here,' she said. 'That is what matters.'

Prison was the same as it ever was.

They arrived just behind a woman with three young children. While the guard checked her papers at the gate, she stubbed her cigarette out on the wall and then put the butt back in her bag for later.

Danny handed over the Visiting Order and Oma's pension book as proof of identity. He filled in a form with their names and address and the guard gave them a ticket with a number on. Danny was too young to visit on his own, and had to be accompanied by an adult. In reality, though, he could have coped easily enough. It was Oma who needed looking after.

They were early, so they sat in the Visitors' Centre, which as usual was full of women and rampaging children. Oma sat humming one of her tunes to herself. She didn't seem aware of the surroundings. She was going to see her son again. That was all that mattered, and she was happy because of it.

Danny sat with her for a time, then went and looked at some leaflets. *Talking to Children about Imprisonment.* He recognized that one. He skimmed through it.

'It is important that they do not see them as a bad person, even if they did do something wrong . . .'

Ha! That was his favourite line in that one. But what if the prisoner really *is* a bad person?

He put the leaflet back and went to sit with Oma again. He calmed his breathing, trying to remember some of the relaxation techniques he had been taught.

'Seventy-three.'

He looked at the ticket. That was their number. 'That's us, Oma,' he said, interrupting her happy daydream.

They went through to the next room. Danny handed over his wallet, his keys and his coat to be stored in a locker. He took off his hooded sweatshirt so that one of the guards could pat him down and check his pockets. He opened his mouth to show that it was empty, then kicked off his shoes for them to examine.

By his side, Oma had to go through the same routine, smiling all the time at the rather uncomfortable-looking female prison officer who was removing the old tissues and sweets from her pockets. Shoes and sweatshirt back on, Danny led Oma through the metal detector and past the sniffer dog and its handler.

They emerged in a hall with about thirty small tables arranged with chairs to either side. About half of them were occupied and most already had visitors. The prisoners who didn't all turned expectantly to look at Danny and Oma, then looked away again. Not the people they were expecting. Not *their* visitors.

These men . . . they were murderers, rapists, drug

dealers; men of violence and brutality and yet . . . the look of lost hope on their faces when they saw that the latest visitor was not their own made them seem just like ordinary people.

One face didn't turn away.

One prisoner met Danny's eyes briefly, and then Oma's, a smile breaking out nervously, uncertainly. The 1970s haircut was gone, the hair short, and thin on top. The features were rounder. Where he had been gangly and awkward in the photo, Danny's father had long since grown into his big frame.

He nodded and waved them towards the chairs at his little table, as if they might head elsewhere if he didn't actually invite them to join him.

'Mum,' he said, taking Oma's hand across the table. 'Daniel.' Smiling more comfortably now, nodding, excited. 'It's been a long time. I didn't know if you'd make it.'

'My boy,' said Oma. 'It is hard since she moved us back of the beyond. Is a long journey on the train and then the bus. Is much for the boy.'

Danny and his father exchanged a look, both smiling at Oma's good-natured grumbling.

It was so easy to forget at times. Despite the guards, the wailing babies and over-excited children, the ever-present low buzz of urgent conversation, just briefly, every so often, Danny and his father could exchange a look, a few words, and they were just father and son. All so natural.

And yet, this was his father: sitting here in this badly

fitting prison uniform. It sometimes seemed that there had been an awful mistake.

But Danny knew there had been no mistake.

This place was where his father belonged.

'How is she?' said his father now. No need to explain the 'she' he referred to. It was Val – his wife, Danny's mother, the 'she' who had moved Danny and Oma away from London when the stresses of trying to live where everyone knew what had happened had become too great. Danny's mother had moved them out to the Hope Springs Trust, a centre for alternative living that had grown up round an old school in the West Country.

'She's fine,' said Danny. 'Teaching more classes at the Trust. Helping them sort their accounts out after the last audit. They don't know what's hit them.'

That's the thing about visiting, Danny thought. You visit so that you can talk and so that's what you do: you actually talk. He couldn't remember talking to his father very much . . . before. But now, when they only saw each other so infrequently, they made good use of the time.

'How's your course going?' Danny asked. His father was studying psychology with the Open University. They talked about the course, about the monotony of the daily prison routine, about some of the people his father was doing time with. They talked about Danny, too. About school and the flat, about TV and music and what it was like living in Wishbourne now that they had settled in. The hands on the big wall clock seemed to keep jumping forward as they talked, time swallowing itself up far too quickly.

'My boy,' said Oma at one point. She hardly spoke on these visits. She always seemed happy just to be in the presence of her son. 'Are they looking after you, heh? Are they feeding you well?'

'Mother, their hospitality never fails. I think I will stay on here for a while.'

Oma looked down sharply at this, and then away, her eyes following the movements of a little boy who was playing with a squeaky hammer in a corner of the hall set up as a toddlers' play area.

'Dad, we found something a few days ago.'

His father raised an eyebrow, waiting for Danny to continue.

'A journal. A black-covered, hardback notebook. The dates in it start in December and run out in . . . a few months later. It was in a box from the move. There's still loads of stuff we haven't unpacked from then, even now.'

His father shrugged. 'What is it? Have you read it?'

'I . . . only a little. It's yours. Your writing. It says about what happened. About what you were thinking.'

It was his father's turn to look down now. After a long silence he said, 'What I was thinking? That's not somewhere I want to go. Not ever again. My writing, you say? I don't remember writing a diary.'

He didn't remember much of anything, though. Nothing that he would tell them at his trial. Nothing that he would ever tell anyone since.

'I just thought you should know that we'd found it,' said Danny softly.

'If you think it's important you could send it to Justin Peters.'

Peters had defended Danny's father at the trial. Danny nodded. It was reassuring to have something to do with the thing.

'Oma had a photo of you on a Chopper,' said Danny, forcing brightness into his voice. On the train the picture had been something to torment him, but now it suddenly seemed different. A treasure from the past, something to make them think, and talk, of better times.

Oma reached into the folds of her skirt and moments later she produced the battered old photograph. 'The lady let me bring it in,' she said, beaming.

'Oh boy, that bike!' His father picked up the photo, his hand shaking.

This was one of those moments. Those brief instants when the surroundings melted away and they could have been anywhere, just grandmother, father and son together. Danny squeezed his eyes shut. He knew it couldn't last.

Back home at Hope Springs, late that night, Danny pushed his bedroom door shut and leaned with his back against it.

The room was dark, lit only by the moonlight through the window. Strange shadows, at strange angles, filled the room, the light blue and cold.

He closed his eyes and tried to calm his ragged breathing.

He went and dropped belly down on the bed, face in the pillow so he could barely breathe.

The rage was there, in his belly and in his chest, struggling to burst free. Out in the real world he could control it. That's what he *did*. But here in his room, the door shut, the world asleep . . . sometimes he just had to let it out.

He punched the pillow with the base of his fist, right next to his head. Punched it again, harder this time.

His father. That place.

His mother and her brisk efficiency. The way she shut out everything and had never, not once, spoken about the things that really mattered.

He remembered faces all around him. People taunting him, calling him names – people who had been his friends. And the looks, or rather, the looking away as soon as eye contact had been made.

All of them.

His hand hurt, he was hitting the pillow so hard. The skin stung with friction burns.

Music. Out in the hallway . . .

It was Oma, humming one of her old German folk tunes. Calming sounds. She always knew.

He stopped thumping the bed. He slid his hand under his belly, now fully aware of the pain. He turned his face on one side, away from the damp patch where he had been sobbing, and stared out at the dark shapes of the trees.

Soon he was asleep.

2

Reminders

But Danny's sleep was both brief and disturbed. He rolled from side to side, tangling himself in the sheets. He dreamed of the prison . . . His father smiling and laughing . . . As if everything were okay.

He woke.

It was dark, only a little after midnight. Images from the dream merged with memories from the day: his father acting as if everything were normal.

How dare he?

Nothing would ever be normal again. Nothing *had* been, since that awful night.

Danny kept a scrapbook.

Or rather . . . not a real scrapbook, as such. Nothing as formal as that. It was just an envelope really. An envelope filled with the past.

He swung his legs out of bed and paused to calm his nerves.

He kept the envelope filled with the past to remind himself. Not that he was ever likely to forget what had happened or what it was like.

He reached out and turned on his bedside lamp. He turned and dropped to his knees on the floor, then hitched the duvet up out of his way and reached beneath the bed. There was a low cardboard box. He slid the box out and it was there: a brown A4 envelope, the address scribbled out with black marker pen.

He took it and sat on the bed, his back against the wall.

Inside, there were yellowed press cuttings, family photographs, a small spiral-bound notepad. He emptied the envelope and lay its contents out on the bed by his side.

He opened the notepad and flicked through it. Only a few pages had been used, the rest left blank. A social worker had urged the eleven-year-old Danny Smith to write down his feelings and draw things. She had said it would help.

The handwriting was big, the lettering carefully sloping in classroom italic. The date was double-underlined, followed by a colon and a dash.

10 October:- School. 10/10 in Maths. Mr Peters says Dad will plea giulty when they ask him next week. He says thats the best thing. Mum is being strong. Oma is organizing us. Since Great-Aunt Eva past away Oma has taken over everything. She's very good at it. Next door is being kind. Everything is AOK, considering.

Beneath that entry, filling up the rest of the page, there was a drawing of Danny, his mother and Oma, all holding hands under a tree that was shedding its red and gold leaves. All were smiling. His mother had her free hand on her tummy, swollen with what was to be Josh.

Danny hadn't been stupid, even back then.

They had wanted him to write down things he would never say to them in person. They had wanted him to draw things that might have exposed the pain and confusion that filled his head every minute of the day, and every minute of every dark, dark night.

They had wanted him to expose the workings of his mind. To open himself up to them.

But he wouldn't do that.

He didn't trust them and he hadn't asked for their help. The social workers, the so-called friends who would just as likely end up selling their inside stories of the Slaughter Family to the papers. The psychiatrist, Dr Jessop, who had understood better than most.

Danny had written what they wanted to read. He had written what might just shut them up.

He hadn't written what it was like to start at high school shortly before your father is due to be tried for a multiple murder. You go there, and there are people and faces you know from junior school, but most you've never seen before because they've come from loads of different schools, and some of your friends from junior school have gone to another high school altogether.

So most of the people there were strangers, but everyone knew Danny.

Word got round quickly.

They looked, they pointed, they talked in hushed tones

so that he only heard enough to know they were talking about him – about his father.

Worse were the ones who looked and then immediately looked away again. Faces pale, turning from him, eyes averted.

As if he might be a chip off the old family block.

As if they didn't want him to notice them, just in case . . .

The neighbours had never been kind to them, despite what Danny told the social workers in his diary. One side, the Walkers, never said a word. Old Mr Sabbatini on the other side was worse. He took to confronting Danny's mother whenever he saw her, asking in his soft but persistent voice when she would be leaving, as she and her kind were a blight on house prices.

None of this went into Danny's spiral-bound notepad, of course. Give them what they want, but don't give them anything of yourself. Lock everything up inside your head. Keep it all in check. That was the way to get through.

He closed the notepad. On the front cover, in the same neat hand, was written *Daniel Smith aged ~~11~~ 12.*

Photographs.

There was a picture of Danny, aged seven or eight, with his father. They were sitting side by side on the swings in the local park, back when they had lived in Loughton. Both had that family look: the dark eyes, the dark hair, the slightly crooked smile, higher on the left than on the right.

Another showed them in a large group on the seafront at Brighton, the pier behind them. Danny stood with his mother and Oma. Great-Aunt Eva was there, tall for an old lady, whereas Oma was shorter and frail from her long-standing illness. Eva had been Danny's favourite grown-up since she had arrived from Germany. She had taken to Danny straight away, and had a wicked sense of humour – much as Oma had developed when she had recovered from her illness.

There were the great-uncles, too: Christian and Dieter. They were there with their wives and there were maybe a dozen more faces in the photograph that belonged to cousins whose names Danny had barely known even then. There hadn't been a word from Christian and Dieter since the trouble, much to Oma's distress. Just when the family should have pulled together, her brothers had abandoned them, disowning them and all their problems.

There was Chris Waller, too, a birdwatching friend of Danny's father, who stood out from the crowd with his coppery hair and the binoculars round his neck. Danny remembered that the two of them had slipped away shortly after his father had taken this picture: along the coast to Rye to look for a Pacific Golden Plover that had been spotted that morning.

Another photograph: Danny, about ten years old, dark hair all over the place so that he looked as if he'd been dragged through a hedge.

Up against his chest, Danny was holding a pistol. He remembered its weight in his hands. He remembered holding it up to aim two-handed, trying to line up the sight at the end of the slender muzzle with the notch at the back. The words *Krieghoff Suhl* were engraved on the back of the pistol. It was a Second World War Luftwaffe Luger, carried by German aircrews.

'It is perfectly safe,' Great-Aunt Eva had assured them all. 'They built them to last forever. But a little dirt, a little muck in the . . . how do you say? *Mechanismus*, the mechanism. My little lifesaver has been stuck up for many years. Is little more than a toy now. Here, let me take a photograph of you, Daniel. There! Like a storm trooper!'

The Luger's mechanism may have been jammed for years, but all it had needed, in the end, was cleaning . . .

He came to the newspaper cuttings.

BIRD RAGE KILLER SHOULD BE STRUNG UP, yelled one headline in white letters set against a black banner. COLD AND CALCULATED – THE MIND OF A KILLER, said another.

ACCOUNTANT STALKED VICTIMS

An accountant arrested by police investigating five north-London killings was remanded in custody by magistrates yesterday.

Anthony Smith, 40, of Loughton, north London, was charged with five counts of murder in connection with the deaths, all of which occurred on the night of 18 April. Magistrates remanded Smith in custody until 25 April, when he is due to appear at the Old Bailey for a preliminary hearing.

Smith, nephew of one of the victims, Eva Hoeness, and friend of another, Christopher Waller, was driven to court in a people carrier with blacked-out windows and escorted by three police cars. He was covered in a blanket as he was led into the court building.

During the ten-minute hearing he spoke only to give his name and address . . .

Danny stopped reading it. He knew the words of every one of these reports off by heart.

He looked at the pictures instead. This one showed two worried-looking men, each with an arm round a figure hunched low beneath a blanket. A more distant shot showed them at the centre of a small crowd – some of the onlookers hostile, more merely curious.

Another story included a grainy version of the big group picture at Brighton, blown-up and tightly cropped to show Chris Waller and Great-Aunt Eva, the other two faces in the picture blacked out.

Danny took the cuttings, the photographs and the notepad and arranged them in a neat pile that he then slid into the brown envelope.

He placed the envelope by his side and sat for long minutes, calm and still.

He kept all this to remind himself of how it had been. He kept it to help him stay alert to the dangers, to remember why it was that he must never lose control.

He kept it to help remember just why it was that nothing could ever be normal again.

3

Dear Diary

Sunday morning. Mum and Josh in the kitchen eating toast, one in a high chair, the other eating as she stood and stared out of the window. As usual, the kitchen was spotless apart from this morning's crumbs. Oma had been up late despite yesterday's long journeys, cleaning and organizing as always. No wonder she had slept in.

'Danny. Sleep well? You still look tired. Will you be okay with Josh this morning?'

'Morning, Val.' That was a Hope Springs thing: everyone on first-name terms. It never seemed natural to Danny and his mother, but it had become something of a family joke. About the only one they had. 'No problem. You with me today, Josh?'

The three-year-old spat out a piece of toast and rubbed jam in his ginger hair. 'I want Mummy!'

Danny glanced at Val and shrugged.

'He'll be okay,' she said. She swept the dyed-red hair back from her face and spread her arms. 'How do I look?' she asked.

She was a short woman, slim, with pale blue eyes. She was wearing yellow leggings and a cropped, tie-dyed top that revealed her newly pierced belly button – a sapphire to match the stud in her nose.

'You look like a middle-aged mother who's trying to be a hippy,' Danny told her.

'You're so sweet.'

'But true.'

'Wish me luck with the hostas.'

'Luck with the hostas.' That was what they called the people who came to study at HoST, the Hope Springs Trust. Stockbrokers and teachers and bankers spending a weekend learning how to do yoga, how to grow vegetables by the cycles of the moon, how to employ the healing powers of crystals. New Age dropouts for the weekend, with their BMWs and Volvos clogging up the car park, and their mobile phones in their pockets just in case anyone from the real world needed to contact them.

She had gone. Off to teach the bankers yoga in one easy morning.

Danny brushed the hair back from his eyes and turned to his young brother.

'Daddy?' said Josh as he was lifted from his high chair. Or it might have been 'Danny', of course.

'Good of you to ask,' said Danny. 'As nobody else seems interested. I thought no one was going to mention it. Yes, I saw Dad yesterday, Josh. He's locked up in prison where he belongs, so that the rest of us are safe from him. He seems okay. He seems ... *adjusted*, which is probably all you could ask for.'

He didn't ask about you, though, young Joshua. I think

he might even have forgotten that you exist. He must have tried hard enough.

They spent the morning in the glasshouses behind the Hall. Danny did his best to help David, the Trust's founder, with the potting of seedlings and at the same time keep Josh out of too much trouble in the compost.

Over lunch, Oma reminded Danny of his father's journal.

'So,' she said to him, over a cup of milky tea. 'Have you wrapped it up for Mr Peters yet?'

Danny knew immediately what she meant by the word 'it'. 'I've been looking after Josh all morning,' he said uncomfortably.

Oma glanced at the toddler and made a clicking sound with her tongue. She had never been close to Josh. She was always telling Val to be stricter with him.

'*She* should be doing that,' she said now. 'Is her responsibility.' She returned to the subject. 'So. You are wrapping it this afternoon, then. No?'

Danny didn't answer.

He hated the thing and the feelings it stirred in him. He didn't want to go anywhere near it. But on the other hand, it would be a relief to be rid of it.

They had come across it in one of the boxes in Josh's room the previous weekend. They had been in this flat at Hope Springs for around six months now, but for some reason these four boxes had remained untouched. It wasn't until Oma had suggested that they finish the unpacking that it had struck Danny quite how odd this should be. Oma was normally so efficient about organizing the household, and yet these boxes had been left sealed.

It was only when he opened the first box that he realized why.

They were his father's things. The few possessions of his that they had brought with them. Some of his books: the two big volumes of the *Concise Birds of the Western Palearctic*, a *Moths of the British Isles*, some volumes of poetry by Ralph Waldo Emerson and Walt Whitman. There were his binoculars and a couple of hardback notebooks small enough to fit in a pocket – the kind he used to take with him when he went birdwatching, to note down his observations.

And a larger notebook, so much like the little pocket-books that Danny almost overlooked it.

But no, it was as if he were meant to find it. His eyes had been drawn back to it and he saw that it was different. As soon as he opened it, he realized that it was a diary, each date double-underlined, followed by a colon and a dash, and then several lines of tiny handwriting. Apart from the handwriting, it looked just like Danny's entries in his own diary, which he kept in the envelope under his bed. Like father, like son. From the very first entry, Danny knew what these pages would contain.

He had slammed it shut immediately. He didn't want this. He didn't want those old wounds to be opened up again. He didn't want to be that close to what had happened. But at the same time ... he was drawn to it, he couldn't resist.

Opening it would do no harm. Reading it.

24 December:– 'Tis the season to be jolly. Ho ho ho. Wrapping presents with Val tonight. My head! It's hurting. Bursting. I'm writing this down. Is it any use? I don't know. I've got to let it all out somehow or I'll burst.

He had read more of it, but then had shut it again, dropped it back in the box and fled the room. He couldn't face it. And yet, ever since, he had been drawn back to it. Perhaps if he read more of it he would begin to understand his father's madness.

It was as if there were a small voice, urging him to read it . . .

Now, Danny looked at Oma and nodded. 'Yes,' he said. 'I'll get it ready. I'll go to the post office with it at lunchtime tomorrow.'

'Good, good, good. I give you the money for posting,' said Oma. 'I get it from *her*.'

All the boxes were still there in Josh's room, packing tape stuck roughly back in place. Last weekend they had got no further in unpacking them once they found the journal.

Danny took the large notebook and went back to his own room. He sat in the wooden window seat with the view over the crowded car park, and stared at the journal's cover. There was nothing to identify it, no label or title, just the words *Guildhall* and *A4 ruled* in the bottom right-hand corner.

18 January:– They think I don't know but I do. I see things. I watch them. I know all about what's going on. Sometimes it's in my dreams. I see what's happening. I watched them today. Tonight, I mean. Saw what they were up to. I followed them. It was meant to be like this. Preordained. He told me all about them. Hodeken tells me all kinds of things. He told me where they'd be tonight.

He remembered that bit from last Sunday – the entries he had managed to read before the memories it stirred became too painful. They were the writings of a madman. A man with imaginary voices in his head. And that madman was his own father, his own flesh and blood. Half of his genes had come from that man. So was he, Danny, half a madman?

16 February:– Voices in my head. It's driving me mad. It's like my skull's splitting open from the inside. They're talking to me. Laughing at me. Telling me what to do. I'll have their tongues. That'll shut them up.

They had never claimed that he was mad, though. If they'd said he was mad he would have been sent to a secure hospital instead of prison and there might have been a chance he could be cured and then they'd have had to set him free. So, no, the prosecution had said he was bad, not mad, and Danny's father had not argued with that.

He *was* mad, of course. Anyone who had done what he had done *must* be mad.

Maybe if they had read this journal they would have treated him differently.

20 March:– SHUT UP!!!!!

Danny closed the book. His vision was blurred. He couldn't read the thing.

He wished he'd never found the diary.

As he had read those words, he could hear his father's voice, as if he were reading them aloud. He put his hands to his face, and squeezed it between them as hard as he could. As if that would shut out his father's voice, the madness in his words.

He remembered his relaxation lessons. The tightening and relaxing of every tiny muscle in his body, one after the other. The breathing. Breathe in, hold, breathe out and hold. Emptying his mind of thoughts. Squashing each new thought as it sparked.

He was in control.

Danny was in control.

Danny was always in control.

He had to be.

The alternative was too terrifying to consider.

He opened his eyes and saw that the journal had slid off his lap and fallen to the floor. He went over to his desk and gathered up the roll of parcel tape and the brown paper he had brought up earlier.

He kneeled. He spread the wrapping paper and placed the journal at the top of the sheet in the middle. Even now, he felt compelled to open it again, to read it and learn where his father had gone wrong.

Instead, he folded it over within the paper, and then folded it over again, and one final time, before folding in one end. Trapping the flap with his knee, he cut off a strip of tape and stuck the paper down. He then repeated this for the other end.

It was a well-wrapped parcel. It made him feel better that the book was so well contained.

He copied the address of the chambers from his mother's personal organizer using a black felt-tip. He realized that he had not enclosed a letter to explain the parcel's contents, but he was sure that his father's barrister would see immediately what this was.

He slipped the parcel into his school bag, placed the tape and organizer on his desk, and then rushed into the bathroom to be sick.

Danny dreamed that night.

He lay awake in his bed for what seemed like hours. His head was spinning, and whenever he closed his eyes he saw rows of tiny handwriting, twisting and swirling before him.

When he woke, he realized that he was squeezing his eyes tightly shut, but then he seemed to have forgotten how to relax those tiny muscles that controlled his eyelids and they remained sealed. No matter how hard he tried, he could not open his eyes.

There was a weight on his chest, too. Not a great

weight, he could still breathe with ease. But a pressure, a presence. Something pressing softly down.

If he could open his eyes he would be able to see what it was.

He felt the panic rising. Like a balloon inflating. Soon, surely, it must burst.

If only he could open his eyes.

A voice: *I can help you, Danny. You just need to open up.*

He opened his eyes and it was still dark. There was nothing on his chest, no soft, insistent voice. All of that had still been the end of a dream.

All that remained was the sense of panic.

Out on the landing, or maybe in the kitchen, Oma was still moving about. She was humming softly, just loud enough for the tune to drift into Danny's room.

He rolled on to his side, and tried to settle.

If he dreamed again that night, he did not recall it in the morning.

4

Cassie

Danny woke and washed and dressed and shoved today's books into his school bag. He looped the ready-knotted tie over his head and tightened it, leaving his top button undone. He pulled on the purple blazer that was too small for him. Because he grew out of things so quickly he was reluctant to ask his mother for another one quite yet. He went through to the kitchen and chucked Josh under the chin, then regretted it immediately as his brother had been trying to eat Weetabix and had spread it all over his face and also, Danny saw, over Oma's beautifully clean floor. She had been scrubbing the tiles again in the night. He washed the gunk off his hand and then wiped the floor. He made himself coffee and toast and glanced at his mother, who was sitting at the table, checking through some notes.

In the five minutes or so that it took Danny to feed himself, the three of them didn't exchange a single word. Mornings were like that sometimes. It wasn't an uncomfortable thing, just how they worked.

He went down the narrow stairs to the door and soon was out into another misty spring morning.

The usual group heading for school was a short distance down the main driveway. Danny would catch them up soon. No reason to hurry.

Hope Springs was based in an old school, Wishbourne Hall. David, HoST's founder, had actually been the headmaster of the school at the time it closed. When the last pupil had left, he had managed to convince the owners to turn the place into an educational trust, and so the old school buildings had been converted into houses and flats and accommodation for visitors, and the grounds had been turned over to assorted experiments in sustainable living. They had solar panels on all the roofs and a reed-bed garden to process the sewage. HoST had actually been thriving for several years, but their accounts were in such a mess that they hadn't quite realized it until Danny's mother had come along and sorted them out.

This place had welcomed them: the people unquestioning and friendly. Nobody here judged them, not that they knew there was anything to judge. It had been such a change, after struggling on for three years in a north-London estate where everyone knew exactly what Danny's father had done, and seemed to think that anyone associated with him must be nearly as bad in some way.

The towering lime trees that lined the drive were in leaf, and at their feet there was a carpet of bluebells in full bloom. Birds sang, butterflies danced through the misty sunlight.

All that stuff was supposed to be uplifting, Danny knew, but his mind was stuck on the journal, now sitting in its brown paper wrapping in the bag slung from his shoulder.

His father's dark secrets. His father's darkest thoughts.

He wanted to be rid of it.

He wanted to read it.

He wanted to run through the village to the bridge, pull the parcel from his bag and sling it into the brook.

By the time he reached the gates, Danny was only a short distance behind the others.

'Hey, Danny,' said David's son, Rick. Shorter than Danny by a head, they all called him Little Rick, although once they were at school they had to remember to call him Mr Sullivan, or just 'sir'.

'Hi, Rick,' said Danny, nodding and fiddling awkwardly with the strap on his shoulder.

There were three others in the group. Tim was red-haired and spectacled and nearly as tall as Danny, although he was only Year Eight. His older brother, Will, who everyone called Won't, was blond and chubby and shorter. Each claimed to be the spitting image of his father. And there was Jade, who was in the Lower Sixth, and was golden-haired and beautiful and made Danny's skin burn every time she talked to him.

The group rounded the bend by the Wishbourne Inn, lost in a Monday morning gloom only broken by Tim and Won't arguing about the weekend's football results. Naturally enough, they supported different teams.

'So where were you and Oma Schmidt on Saturday, then?' asked Rick, smoothing his black ponytail and squinting at Danny in the morning light. 'Out all day, not back till late.' He pronounced Oma Schmidt rapidly, all as one word: Omaschmidt. It sounded funny and wound Oma up, at which Danny couldn't help but laugh sometimes.

He shrugged now. 'Just out for the day,' he said. 'Back to London. Visiting.' No one needed to know any more than that. *Just visiting*.

They crossed the bridge over the brook and turned right on to the lane across the fields to Grafton-on-Severn.

A short distance ahead of them was another small group – girls from the other side of the village.

'So what's your sign then, Danny?' asked Won't, in a silly high voice.

'This,' said Danny, raising his middle finger.

One of the girls was Cassie Lomax, and last week, one lunch break, she had asked Danny what his star sign was. 'I . . . I don't know,' he had lied, not aware that Won't and some of the others were listening.

She had narrowed her too-wide eyes, and then said, 'Virgo, I reckon.' Wrong. He was Libra, although it was all nonsense. 'You not going to ask what I am?' she had said, and then laughed when he shook his head.

Now she looked back along the track, just briefly. Her wild, dark hair made her look like she hadn't brushed it in weeks, although she was always fussing over it so he knew that wasn't true. She was skinny and frighteningly clever and . . . He was watching her, he realized.

She glanced back again, and he looked down, away. He adjusted the strap of his bag and remembered the parcel.

Lunchtime seemed so far away, and he was going to have to carry this thing around school with him all morning.

He was tempted to slip away right then, and go straight to the post office but, friendly as Little Rick was, he wouldn't turn a blind eye to Danny bunking off.

When he looked up again, the girls had merged with the other groups on the way to Severnside Community School.

'Have a good day, Danny,' said Little Rick.

'Have a good day, sir,' said Danny, and they went in through the front gates.

'You have posted it?' asked Oma.

Danny had the sense that she had been waiting all day to ask him this. She had been in the grounds of Hope Springs when he returned from school, fussing with some pots on the track by the lake.

He nodded, and couldn't help but smile at her satisfied look.

'That is good,' she said.

'What's so good about it?' said Danny. The only good thing, as far as he was concerned, was that the diary was no longer in the flat. The weight of its dark contents had lifted.

'It puts things right,' said Oma. 'Is truth.'

But it was too late to change things, thought Danny, although he knew better than to upset his grandmother. It was far too late to change anything.

'All I want,' she said now, 'is to bring the family together. You think that bad? You want me to give up that hope that I have? You tell me to stop, I stop. You tell me to go, I go.'

She did this sometimes. They all did: Oma, Danny, his father. They could switch, just like that, from happy to sad, from calm to angry. One moment she had been buzzing like the bees in Little Rick's hives, and now she was upset, as if she realized how futile it was to hope for a happy family ever again.

'Of course we don't want you to stop, or go anywhere. What would we do without you?' He kicked at a stone on the path, awkward, knowing that she had trapped him into saying things. *Go on, tell me you love me!*

She was smiling now.

'I only keep going because my family needs me. So tell me, Daniel Schmidt: you want things how they were?'

Danny nodded. If only ... 'Yes, I'd love things to be how they were.'

They walked back towards their flat in the main school building. Luke, one of the founding members of the Trust, was bent over in the undergrowth, hauling at the ground elder. When they passed him, Oma nudged him in the backside. Instantly, she bounded off like a ten-year-old.

Danny looked at Luke, sprawled in the weeds and then at Oma's retreating figure, and then he was after her. Round the corner of the old chapel, they stopped, gasping for air, giggling like little children. 'Is funny, *ja*? He stick his fat ass in the air like that – what does he expect?'

★

Tuesday afternoon, Danny trailed out of the school gates, loosening his tie. He headed up Morses Lane, and then turned right on to the track that followed Carrant Brook back over the fields to Wishbourne.

A wood pigeon flew across the track and up into the willows that lined the brook to his left, then immediately it changed its mind and flew off again.

He walked to one side of the track, avoiding the puddles in the ruts left by the wheels of farm vehicles.

Cassie Lomax was ahead of him. Alone, just as he, too, was alone.

They weren't completely on their own, of course. There were groups ahead of Cassie on the track, and Danny could hear voices from behind. They seemed very distant, though.

She was dangling her bag so that it almost dragged along the ground at her side, the long straps bunched up in her right hand. Her bare calves flashed pale in the afternoon sunlight as she walked.

Danny kept looking down, looking away from her, as if someone somewhere might be watching him.

Watching him watching her.

He felt his heart thumping and he made himself breathe more slowly, more calmly. At lunchtime he'd seen her with Kate Jordan and Jo Lee, talking and laughing. He hadn't heard what they were talking about. He hadn't wanted to get too near, in case they thought he was weird.

Halfway along the track, Cassie paused and glanced back over her shoulder. She'd seen him now, he was sure.

She was going to wait for him. Probably ask him something stupid about his star sign or whatever. Or ask him why he'd been watching her at lunchtime, even though he was certain she hadn't noticed him.

When he looked back up, she was still walking. She wasn't going to wait for him after all. Wasn't going to ask him something stupid.

He realized that he was disappointed. He felt very alone at the moment. But he was relieved, too.

He watched her: the way that she walked, the way she dangled her bag.

She looked back again. She was smiling.

Was she playing games with him? Winding him up?

At the end of the track she turned right, away from Hope Springs, and so did Danny.

He was keeping his distance, and the kink in the road by the old railway line took her from his sight for a time. Long enough for him to wonder what on earth he was doing and then to squash that thought like an ant. He came round the high walls of the garden of Forge Cottage and she was there, ahead of him. Closer now: either she had slowed or he had quickened his pace when he had lost sight of her.

She looked up, not quite back at him, and turned down Swiss Lane. She must live in one of the wooden chalet-houses, he thought. Someone had once said they were so badly built that no one could ever get a mortgage on them. That's what they meant by 'the other side' of Wishbourne: the council houses and chalets.

He came to the top of the lane, lost in thought.

'Are you following me or what?'

He gasped as she emerged from a gap in the hedge. He stood and stared at her. There must be a convincing answer, other than 'yes', but he couldn't think of it right now.

'I say hel-lo. *Comprenez-vous?* Anyone at home up there?'

She was standing with her hands on her hips, leaning forward, head jutting.

'I . . . um . . .'

'Joking. That's what I'm doing: getting a rise.' She patted him on the arm, like an adult humouring a child. 'I ask what you're doing and you're like . . .' She let her jaw drop and pulled a goofy expression.

'So what brings you to the posh side of the village?'

'I . . . the shop.' He gestured with his head as he spoke, nodding in the direction of the village store.

'And I thought it was me.'

He stared.

She laughed. 'Me going to the shop, I mean. We could go together, hey? Make an outing of it.'

He walked with her, wondering what she was up to, what game she was playing. Why was she treating him like this? Pretending to find him interesting when he said barely a word. Smiling and laughing and chattering away.

In anybody else it would be a character flaw to be so suspicious of everyone, but for Danny it was natural. It was how he survived. He didn't trust anyone else, and he didn't trust himself. He was always on his guard. It got him through.

'Last of the great talkers, are you?'

'Not much to talk about.'

'Nobody sees the world through your eyes. Nobody knows all the things that you know. What's in your head, chatterbox? Everyone's got something to talk about. I'm like, listen to me! Maybe I'm the odd one: I have a thought and I have to share it. I talk less, you talk more, how about that? So what's in your head, big boy?'

'Nothing.' He shook his head. They had stopped by the shopfront, while Cassie prattled on. 'There's nothing special in my head. I'm just ordinary. Same as everyone else.'

She looked at him, eyes wide, smirking. 'Oh, how dull,' she said, and turned and went into the shop, leaving the door to swing shut against him as he followed.

A short time later, back at the top of Swiss Lane, she turned to him and said, 'I'm sorry if I surprised you, waiting in the hedge like that. Don't mind me. I'm mad, me.'

She doesn't know what mad is, Danny thought. She can't even begin to know.

5
The Start of It All

Back home, when Danny had finished his homework, he sat and ate a chilli con soya while his mother drank red wine and Oma grumbled about the spiciness of the food.

Danny sat quietly. Calmly.

A sound came from the bottom of the stairs up to the flat. It was the clunk of the door.

'Hello?' Little Rick's muffled voice came up the stairwell. 'Can I come up?'

Val hurried across the landing and leaned over the railing, gesturing Rick up. 'Shush,' she said softly. 'Josh is asleep.'

Rick walked into the kitchen-diner. 'Sorry,' he said. 'I hope I haven't woken him.'

He pulled up a chair and sat at the table.

Oma clicked her tongue disapprovingly. 'She leaves the front door open like I tell her not to,' she muttered, poking at the rice with her fork.

'It's okay,' said Val. 'We're not in London now. Things are a lot more laid back here at Hope Springs.'

'Hi, Danny,' said Rick. 'Hi, Oma Schmidt.' *Omaschmidt.*

She clicked her tongue again, and Danny smirked, then stopped himself.

'Luke's been printing posters for the open day,' Rick said. 'They look good. There are going to be ads in the *Crier* and *Echo*, too. It's about time we tried to pull the local community into Hope Springs. It's all very well us doing our sustainable thing in isolation, but we need to send ripples out into the real world if we're ever going to change anything.'

'It'd be nice if they didn't just see us as cranks,' said Val, pouring herself some more red wine and a fresh glass for Rick.

'What was it Schumacher said in *Small Is Beautiful* – he didn't mind being called a crank because cranks cause revolutions?' Rick raised his glass, chinked it with Val's, and drank.

Danny watched, and wondered about the two of them.

His mother was even more suspicious of people than Danny was, and Oma was hostile to anyone who intruded on what she considered family territory. They must be a difficult family to penetrate.

Rick didn't seem to notice, or to care. He called in quite often to talk with Danny or Val.

Maybe he was like this with everyone. Danny wasn't sure. Maybe sometimes he just wanted to talk to someone other than David and his father's partner, Sharmila.

Rick said something that Danny didn't catch. Danny looked down at his food.

He felt sick, he realized. Deep in the pit of his belly. Things were changing . . . something new starting. Ever since he had found that journal, things had felt different.

He thought of Cassie. Of how she had waited for him behind the hedge at the top of Swiss Lane. How she had stepped out, startling him.

But she could only have waited for him because he was already following. Stalking her.

He shut out the thought. He had to keep control.

He took another mouthful of the chilli, but somehow the flavour had vanished.

Later, in his room, he sat in the window seat.

It was dark outside. No moon or stars; no street lights out here in Wishbourne. The flat was too far from the road to be penetrated by the headlights of any passing cars. Just darkness.

He stared into the glass of his window and a shadowy version of himself stared back. He studied the dark eyes, the pale features, all distorted in the old glass.

His father had stalked his victims. Eva and Chris, at least. Everyone accepted that the other three had 'merely' been in the wrong place at the wrong time. He had stalked Chris Waller several times before the night when it all happened.

Danny closed his eyes and saw Cassie. Ahead of him on the track, bag dangling, glancing back. She'd been leading him on. Wanting him to do something.

And he had followed her.

Was this how it had started?

His father's journal had spoken of voices in his head. Voices that goaded him, leading him on. All kinds of voices, but the main one had belonged to someone he called Hodeken: some kind of personal demon. Hodeken had gone on and on at him, telling him what to do, taunting him when he did not do as he was told. It was Hodeken's voice that Danny's father had been trying to stop when he cut out his victims' tongues.

Danny heard voices.

Inside his head, inside the barricades of his skull, he talked to himself all the time ... his own voice bouncing around inside his head. Other people's voices, too: his father, Val, Oma, Won't and Tim taunting him. Cassie Lomax's 'Virgo, I reckon.' He remembered the intense urge to read more of his father's journal that had built up from within, a pressure driving him on, nagging at him – not so much a voice, but an urge that had been almost irresistible ...

Was this what it had been like? Or was everybody like this? Was everyone a ball of anger and frustration, tightly controlled, just waiting to be let loose?

There had been a dream ... a dream of a nagging voice telling him to trust it, to open up. But, no: that had just been a dream, nothing more. He was *not* going to end up like his father.

He looked at the window, staring right through his shadow self into the darkness. His pulse was steady, his breathing calm.

He met his own eyes again. *Just what are you capable of, Daniel Smith?*

His reflection didn't answer, which he thought was probably just as well.

6
Two Telephone Calls

His father called on Friday after school.

Danny, alone in the flat, took the call. Oma was out in the greenhouses, Val was leading a meditation session in the old chapel and Josh was with one of the other Hope Springs parents.

He picked up the phone and said, 'Yuh?' He wandered through to the living room and sat with his feet over the side of the chair.

'Danny, it's me.'

Danny froze, then gathered himself. 'Dad,' he said. 'How's it going?'

'As ever,' said his father. 'Well, no, actually. That's not quite true. I have some news.'

At these words, Danny tensed as if a pulse of static electricity had buzzed across his skin, his scalp. News. His father never had news. He felt as if he were in a crowded room, everyone waiting for the next words.

'Hmm?'

'That book you found. The journal. Mr Peters got it on Wednesday. Thanks for that. He came to see me today. He says it throws everything into a new light. He says that if they'd had that as evidence when they were assessing me things would have gone differently. He thinks it might be enough evidence to appeal on the grounds that I was never in a fit state to be tried in the first place.'

'You mean . . . he's going to get you out?'

'No, not get me out.'

He did do it, after all. Danny's father had killed five people, three of them simply because they had been in the way. There had never been any question of that.

'But I might go to a hospital instead. They might be able to treat me for . . . for whatever it is that went wrong.'

Danny was silent. This was the closest his father had ever come to talking about what had happened to him that night, and in the weeks leading up to it. He wasn't sure if that was good or not. Some things might be best left unprobed.

'You still there, Danny?'

'I'm still here.'

'You're not pleased?'

'I'm not anything.' It was all going to be stirred up again. Wounds reopened.

If only they had left those boxes undisturbed. If they had not found the journal there could be no chance of an appeal.

'Listen, Danny. Hold on in there. Do you hear? There's not much time left on my phonecard. I'll call again when I get another one. Are you okay, Danny?'

'I'm okay.' But by then he was talking to a dead line, his father's card having run out.

*

He had to say something, but he wasn't sure how.

'Dad called,' he said finally. The simple option.

Val looked up from her salad, then back down again. Oma watched him carefully.

'He says Mr Peters thinks he has grounds for appeal.'

Val speared a slice of boiled egg, then let it drop.

Oma was beaming, clasping her hands together as if giving thanks to the heavens. 'Is happy day,' she said. '*Ja?*'

Nobody said anything.

'You get your wish, Danny,' Oma continued. 'You wish things could be how they were. You remember? Like old times. The family together. All happy. *Ja?*'

Things could never be how they were. Was she blind to that? Couldn't she understand what her son had done? Danny was about to point out that his father wasn't going to be set free, just like that, but Val got in first.

She gave a kind of strangled grunt as she stood from the table, knocking her chair back against the sideboard. Startled by the sudden loud noise, she looked to the doorway in case it had woken Josh. Then she put her hands to her face and gasped, 'No.'

Tears ran through her fingers, and across the backs of her hands. 'No,' she said again. 'Can't you see? How could we ever be happy families again?'

Oma rose and went across to her. She made a little beckoning gesture and held her arms wide. When Val didn't move, she went to her and took her in her arms. She started to hum one of her German folk tunes, and instantly the atmosphere grew calmer.

She looked at Danny and winked, as if they two shared

a secret. She really seemed to think that this was the start of a *new* start, that things could somehow get back to how they were.

Danny went to his room and opened his envelope to remind himself why that could never ever be so.

Saturday mid-morning and the phone went again. They didn't get many calls here. Their friends were mostly within Hope Springs, and they didn't need to use the telephone to talk to them.

Danny answered. He half expected it to be his father again, with the latest developments, although it was unlikely anything would have happened at the weekend.

'Yuh?'

'Hello, could I speak to Danny Smith, please?'

'Speaking.'

'Danny. You sound different on the phone. It's me, Cassie Lomax.'

Danny's mother was mouthing, *Who is it?* He put a hand over the phone and said, 'A friend.' She raised an eyebrow, and returned to cleaning Josh.

Danny went into the living room with the phone. 'What was that?' he said, as Cassie had carried on talking during his exchange with Val.

'I *said*, I'm out in the village right now and it's lovely and sunny and I'm like, let's call Danny and see what he's doing. You want to come out? I mean, not *go out*. I'm not asking you on a date or anything. I mean, it's nice and I thought you might want some fresh air, and I can talk too much and you can do your strong silent bit and all that. A right pair, we are. I'm down in the church car park right now. What do you reckon?'

He was smiling. He'd held the phone away from his ear while she talked, listening to her from a distance. He'd never known anyone like Cassie Lomax.

'Okay,' he said. 'Five minutes.'

'Okay. Five minutes.'

He pressed the disconnect button on the phone's handset, and leaned back in his chair.

A few minutes later he was heading out down the main driveway, past the lime trees and bluebells.

7
What Parents Do

The church was right next to Hope Springs. The community's grounds were enclosed by a two-metre-high wall, which formed one side of the triangular church car park. The road formed the second side and the vicarage railings the third. The entrance to the churchyard was at the top of the triangle, and Cassie was sitting on one of the benches inside the lychgate, in the shade of its roof.

'Just as well it's not a date, cos I haven't made much effort,' she said, coming out into the sunlight. She was wearing a baggy green T-shirt, and jeans that were faded down the front and dark on either side. 'So, where are we going, then?'

Danny stood there, mouth partly open. 'I . . .'

She laughed. 'Come on,' she said. 'Take me through the grounds of the school. I've never been there. I want to see if it's like they say.'

When she said 'school' she meant Hope Springs. Villagers still called it Wishbourne Hall School, even though it had been run by HoST for something like ten years now.

'What do they say it's like?'

She was past him already, so Danny turned and trotted to catch up.

'You're all naturists,' said Cassie. 'And devil worshippers, of course. You dance naked under the full moon and sacrifice babies to The Dark One Below. You grow pot in the greenhouses, too. And there's lots of brainwashing going on all the time, of course. That's what you're like. It's what everyone says so it has to be true, doesn't it?'

'Through here,' Danny pointed to a small trail through the trees, cutting away from the main driveway.

'So what's it like, then? Living in a commune. Does everyone wear sandals and have long beards and things?'

'Only the women,' said Danny. 'It's not a commune, really. It's an experiment in sustainable living. We recycle everything we can. We grow a lot of our own food. We treat our own sewage and generate our own electricity. People come from all over the world to learn from Hope Springs.'

They passed some houses. 'These are all private homes,' Danny told her. 'Nothing to do with Hope Springs. When the school closed down they sold off some of the land for building and put the money into the Hope Springs Trust.'

They came to a clearing in the trees. From here, they could look over the vegetable plots to the main school building, Wishbourne Hall: a solid, red-brick construction with narrow windows that made it look vaguely monastic.

'That's good,' said Cassie. 'I made that eight or nine.'

Danny looked sideways at Cassie. She was waiting for him to ask what on earth she meant. Smirking. He looked down, and walked in silence.

'Sentences,' she said, finally. 'All in a row. Don't stop. Go on – tell me more. I want to know about this place. It's like, another little village stuck slap bang in the middle of Wishbourne. Different rules.'

'We have an open day in a couple of weeks. You're early.'

They came to the lake and followed the path around one side.

'So where are they, then?'

Again, waiting for him to ask what she meant.

He looked at her and raised his eyebrows.

'The springs. It's called Hope Springs. There must be springs.'

Danny had never thought of it like that. 'There's a stream,' he said. 'It runs into the lake. The spring must be up the hill somewhere.'

'So, it's Hope Streams, then, really. Or Hope *Stream*. Not Hope Springs at all. I might come and change it one night, on the sign at the bottom of the drive. Cross out the "Springs" and write "Stream". Just for the sake of accuracy. So what are you doing here? How did you end up in a place like this?'

'Things got tight,' he said. The official version of events, as far as anyone here knew. 'Dad lost his job. We couldn't afford to stay in London. Mum sold up and bought a stake in Hope Springs Trust and a lease on a flat in the Hall.'

'What about your dad?'

Danny stared at her. What did she know? What had she heard?

'You're like, your dad loses his job but it's your mum who sells up and buys into the kooky club. There's a jump there. A gap in your story.'

He swallowed.

'They separated. It's just me, Mum, my gran and my brother, Josh, now.'

One of the willows had a big branch that swept out over the lake where the stream rushed in. Cassie sat astride it with her back against the main trunk.

'Parents,' she said. 'Larkin was right, wasn't he?'

Danny looked at her, lost again. She seemed to know so much more than he did.

'Philip Larkin. The poet. They mess you up. That's what he said parents do. They fill you up with all their faults and then they give you some more, too. Only he said it better than that in the poem. There's a lot of truth in poetry.'

Too much truth, perhaps, thought Danny.

'*There was a crow sat on a plough,*' he recited. '*He hasn't gone, he's still there now.*'

Cassie snorted out a laugh, and shifted so that Danny could sit with her. 'Like I say,' she said, 'a lot of truth. Your crow poses the big question of existence: why are we here? Simple. It's because we haven't gone. Poetry has all the answers.'

'Your parents?'

'Divorced.'

Danny leaned down to pick up a stick, then sat tracing shapes in the water with it.

'Everything was fine,' said Cassie. 'They're still best friends. But one day Dad just announced that he'd decided he was gay and that was it. Not a lot you can say to that. I didn't tell anyone for ages. I used to just tell people he was in prison, but I couldn't do that once he started visiting with his boyfriend. It took a bit of adjusting, but it's cool now. Are you shocked?'

Not shocked, just confused. Thrown off guard. She kept asking difficult questions, saying things that made him uncomfortable, like the claim that her father was in prison. Too close to home. Also, he was aware of how close they were sitting.

He stood. 'Shall we look for the spring?' he asked.

They followed the stream. It was easy enough at first, but then a wide bed of nettles and brambles made them leave its course for a while.

Farther up the hill it ran between two fields, lined on one bank by a barbed-wire fence and on the other by another row of willows. When the going became harder, Cassie kicked off her shoes and went ankle-deep in the water. 'Come on,' she said. 'It's bleeding cold, but it's okay.'

Reluctantly, Danny untied his trainers and removed them, and then his socks. He stepped into the water and yelped. It was like ice, and the stones were hard and bit into his feet like rounded teeth. He danced on to his other foot, and instantly the sensations were repeated.

He backed out of the water.

Cassie came laughing after him, and they sat on the crumbling grassy bank, drying their feet in the sun.

'Know what my name means?'

'Huh?' Danny had been lying back, eyes closed against the bright light. He turned his head and squinted at Cassie.

She had produced some wraparound shades from somewhere and was just putting them on. 'My name,' she prompted him.

'I thought they were calling you "Kathy" at first,' said Danny.

She laughed. 'Yeah. And everyone had a lithp, Mithter Thmith.'

'Cassie. Cassandra? Greek, isn't it? Or Roman.'

'Very good. Cassandra Jeanette Lomax. Daughter of the King of Troy. Cassandra was, that is. She's like, the most drop-dead gorgeous of all his daughters. Okay. You don't have to say anything at this point, Smith. Okay? The god Apollo, he gave her the power of prophecy if she'd like, you know, give him a quick something in return. But she was a tease, was Cassandra. Once she had what she wanted, she dumped the guy, but you don't want to be doing that to a god, so he turned his gift into a curse. He made it so that no one would believe her when she told them something was going to happen, even though she was always right. So she went through her life with no one believing her. She even foretold her own death, but they didn't believe that, either. Damned gloomy name to give your firstborn, if you ask me.'

Danny shifted on the grass, but said nothing.

'So. Aren't you going to ask me to look into the

future? That's what people usually do when I tell them the Cassandra story. You say you're just like everyone else, but you're not asking the obvious question.'

'Maybe I don't want to know the future,' said Danny. It was like the astrology: nonsense. But he liked her talking, even so.

'You know what I think? I think maybe someone's put a spell on you. Maybe even Apollo himself. He's taken your tongue, cursed you to talk in as few words as possible. One day someone will break that spell and you'll start to talk and you'll never stop.'

She had done it again! Another innocent choice of phrase that cut right to the dark depths of his secret past. *I'll have their tongues*, his father's journal had said. He had wanted to stop people talking, stop the voices that plagued him, and so he had removed his victims' tongues.

'You okay?'

'I'm okay. Just some things I'd rather not think about.'

'Okay. You want to kiss me?'

She was looking down at him, leaning on her elbow. She looked nervous, suddenly.

Danny nodded.

'No tongues, mind.' She leaned down and her lips pressed against Danny's.

He didn't know whether to close his eyes or not, so he narrowed them. He saw his own eyes in her shades when she was close. He didn't know whether to breathe or not, but then it was over, and she had pulled back.

'Did it work?' she asked.

He looked at her. This was another one of her questions he didn't understand.

'The kiss breaks the spell. Or at least, it does in the stories. It turns the frog into the handsome prince. It wakens the sleeping princess.'

Another one of her games.

'You're supposed to start talking now that your spell has been broken.'

He shook his head, grinning. He couldn't keep up. 'You know what *my* name means?' he asked. 'Do you know what's special about it?'

'Daniel Smith. Let's see. It's not obvious, is it? There must be a thousand other Daniel Smiths out there. Daniel. Something biblical. Isn't it the name of one of the books in the Bible? They could have called you Leviticus, I suppose . . . And Smith. Someone who makes things. Blacksmith. Locksmith. Silversmith. It means you have traditionalist parents who chose you a good biblical name, and that somewhere in the past you have an ancestor who did things with his hands. Am I right?'

'Maybe. But you missed out what it hides. It's not really Smith – it's Schmidt. Or at least, my gran changed her surname to the English equivalent when she came to England. She came here in the 1960s with her two brothers. They were getting away from the troubles in Berlin. The three of them made it but their sister didn't. She came much later. They didn't know she was still alive, until she turned up on the doorstep one day. She's . . . dead now.'

'Your gran. Is she the one who lives with you now?'

Danny nodded. 'She's a Smith officially, but we still call her "Oma Schmidt" at home. That's German for Grandma Smith.'

Cassie giggled. 'Sounds like an apple! Granny Smith. That's biblical, too: the apple in the Garden of Eden. Temptation. Original sin and all that.'

He was getting used to the way Cassie's mind raced off in so many different directions. Sort of.

Rather than follow the course of the stream back down the hill, they cut through to the track that led down from Moreton Farm.

'You can hold my hand if you like.'

He did. Her hand was tiny in his. It made him think of *Beauty and the Beast*.

'You know what I think?'

She was going to tell him, he was sure. He waited and she continued.

'I think that one day you might actually trust someone enough that you'll open up and tell them all the things you're always so careful to keep locked up inside.'

'I don't believe you, Cassandra. I don't believe anything you tell me about the future.'

She smacked his arm with her free hand.

They came to the gate at the top end of the Hope Springs grounds. Danny opened it and held it for Cassie. Once in the grounds, he didn't take her hand again.

8

Little Rick

Danny found Oma Schmidt in the long glasshouse behind the Hall. Bustling about, gathering disused pots and sorting them into different sizes. Always cleaning, always tidying – that was Oma Schmidt's way.

Danny paused in the doorway. There was something in the set of her shoulders, and the jerky way she moved . . . She seemed upset.

He went in, picking up a terracotta pot. He placed it on the bench where she was working and she clicked her tongue disapprovingly. She snatched it up and reached over to put it on a stack of pots of the same size and then she paused and looked across her shoulder at him.

Instantly she smiled, the tense expression slipping away.

'Ah, Danny, my boy! Good, good. You come to help Oma Schmidt? Everyone, they are on the edge about the open day, you know. They say there has been no village fête for the last four years and the people of the village will be putting up a marquee on the grass and having it here with us.'

Danny knew all this – it had been arranged months before. 'That's good, isn't it?'

'Ach, yes, but it all seems so *disorganized*.'

'It'll be okay.'

'You think?' Oma started to brush off the bench. 'He came round again,' she went on. 'Richard. Little Rick. Can he not see where he is not wanted?'

Danny was puzzled by that. 'But . . .'

Oma looked at him, briefly. 'I do not like him. He makes me shiver. Your mother does not like him either. But still he comes.'

Everybody liked Little Rick. He was popular at Severnside Community School, just as he was popular at Hope Springs. 'Val seems to like him well enough,' he said. 'She needs friends. She needs to start having a life again.'

Oma tensed. She was brushing the same part of the bench over and over, as if trying to get rid of a stubborn mark. 'She had a life before,' she said softly. 'She had a life before but she made it a mess. Splitting the family up with her friends and with her "having a life".'

Danny turned and headed for the door. Oma had always blamed his mother for what had happened. She had always blamed his mother's . . . *friendship* with Chris Waller. She seemed to be blind to what her own son had done as a result, though. To her, it would always be Val's fault that the family had split up.

'Danny? Don't rush off. Don't be cross with old Oma Schmidt. I am a foolish old woman, no more. I am only thinking of the family.'

He stopped.

Instead, he went to check on the plants he'd potted a

few days earlier. The tomatoes were okay, planted directly in the soil with plastic collars round them, but snails had been after the peppers. He'd need to top up the beer traps.

'I saw you with your *Freundin*,' said Oma, in a playful tone.

His German was patchy, but he was pretty sure that meant 'girlfriend'. He said nothing.

'Does she have a name?'

'Cassie,' said Danny. It felt awkward, talking about her like this.

'Is she a nice girl?'

He was hardly going to say 'no' . . . He shrugged, said nothing.

'You be good, Danny. You be careful of where she might lead.'

'There. That's it. Just put it there, Danny. That's right.'

Danny dropped the plywood beehive on an open patch of grass, then shifted it to the left a little so that it was stable.

Little Rick was halfway up a step ladder, wedged into the branches of an apple tree in the Hope Springs orchard. He had his beekeeper's hat and gloves on, but no other protective clothing, despite the seething mass of honeybees wrapped round the trunk of the tree, little more than a couple of metres away.

'Right,' he said. 'Now you need to take the roof and the crown board off.'

Danny lifted the roof and placed it back in the

wheelbarrow Rick had used to move the hive from his store. Beneath it was a flat board with some ventilation holes. He removed this too. In the next level down there was some old honeycomb, the cells still capped over with wax.

Rick reached a hand over, close to the swarm, and encouraged some of the bees to crawl on to his glove.

Slowly, he backed down the steps. He held his hand inside the open hive and the two of them watched as some of the bees crawled on to the frames of honeycomb, while one or two lifted heavily from his glove and flew back up into the tree.

'They're dopey when they're swarming,' said Rick. 'Everyone gets hot and bothered about swarms, but the bees are usually so stuffed full of honey that they can't actually get themselves into position to sting, even if they wanted to.'

Danny glanced up at the chaotic bundle of bees in the tree. He could understand people getting bothered about something like that.

Once the last bee had left his hand, Rick stepped back and dropped the gloves and then his hat into the barrow. He took the crown board and positioned it on top of the open hive, and then the roof. Then he kneeled down before the hive and adjusted the position slightly.

'We can move the hive once they're settled in,' he said. 'Have you ever seen a swarm moving into its new home? It's quite a sight to see.'

'Where's this one going to go?' Danny asked.

'I don't know yet,' said Rick. 'I need to check my

spreadsheet. I've got it all worked out to the finest detail against a plan of the grounds and the surrounding gardens and fields. I try to get the positioning exactly right, so the hives aren't competing with each other. You have to pay attention to detail, don't you?'

One of the bees had found its way down through the brood chambers and out to the entrance block. It sat there in the sunlight for a few seconds, and then lifted into the spring air. Danny watched it fly away, ignoring the swarm altogether.

'It seems so random,' he said. 'Uncoordinated.'

'Each swarm is a single family unit,' said Rick. 'It's like a finely tuned machine, despite appearances. Once the bees in the hive have investigated and approved it, you just watch.'

Just then, a loud yelping cry came from deeper into the orchard.

'Hear that? A spotted woodpecker,' said Rick.

'Green woodpecker,' corrected Danny automatically.

'Of course it is,' said Rick. 'You know your birds, don't you?'

'My father,' said Danny. 'He used to take me bird-watching.' Up to the Lea Valley Country Park to see the bitterns, or maybe down to Dungeness on a twitch with Chris Waller.

'You miss him?'

Danny nodded.

'See him much?'

'When I can. We talk on the phone. It's not the same, though.'

'Of course not,' said Rick. 'It's difficult.'

Danny looked at him, wondering how much he knew, how much Val had given away.

'Listen, Danny, if you ever need someone to talk to, you know I'm here, don't you? Not as a teacher. As a friend.'

'Thanks,' said Danny. More than three years in a family where no one would talk and now twice in two days . . . Yesterday Cassie, and now Rick. Both of them offering listening services, trying to get him to open up and talk.

Was it that obvious? Were the conflicts in his head so obvious that everyone was going to take him on as a sympathy case? He remembered the social worker, earnestly trying to get him to expose his thoughts in a diary.

He didn't need their help. He was coping.

'Know what I think?' asked Rick.

Danny shrugged.

'You're a funny lot, the four of you. There's you, Val and Josh, and then you've got Omaschmidt clinging on. She's not *Val's* mum, is she? Your dad's gone, but his mother stays with you . . . Very peculiar.'

So Val hadn't told him much.

'Oma's always been close to us. We're all she has.'

Rick nodded. 'It's like a swarm without the queen,' he said. 'That's what I think. You have a man-shaped space in your family. That's what I mean when I say, you know, if you need someone to talk to . . .'

'Are you and Val . . . seeing each other?'

Rick narrowed his eyes, still staring up at the swarm.

'You'd better ask Val that,' he said. 'Your mother . . . she's a hard person to get to know. She keeps herself well guarded. Most people that defensive, they have their own good reasons.'

Danny nodded. She had good reason, all right.

'Must be something bad,' Rick continued. Probing, teasing out his own conclusions. 'Your father, I'd guess.'

It was that obvious, despite all their efforts to make a new start.

'It's okay,' said Rick. 'I won't say anything. I won't give your secrets away.' He laughed, suddenly.

'What?' said Danny. What was so funny about all this?

'Sorry. It's true what they say, though, isn't it? You choose your friends but you can't choose your family. Were you close to your father?'

Danny shook his head. 'We're closer now, if anything,' he said. 'At a distance.'

And then he added, 'It's just . . . I try very hard not to be like him.' It was a struggle he fought every minute of every day. Any little sign, any slight indication that he was like his father had to be squashed.

'We're all scared of turning out like our parents,' said Rick. 'Look at David! God, how I'd hate to be like him and live his life. Sad little headmaster of a failing school, too blind to see that it was all unravelling around him. So obsessed with the fine detail of his life that he couldn't see what was really going on. He drove my mother away with his obsessiveness. He couldn't see what he was doing to her. She couldn't stand it.'

'*You're* a teacher,' said Danny. Fairly obsessive, too,

judging by the way he looked after his bees as if it were a military campaign. 'You're following in his footsteps whether you want to or not.'

'But I'm not *him*,' said Rick. 'I'm different. We all are. Okay, so we share some of our genes: I'm half of my father. But humans share something like ninety-nine per cent of their genes with chimpanzees, yet you don't see us jumping around in trees and scratching our hairy backsides. Not most of us, anyway. It's like Mozart and Robbie Williams: they use all the same musical notes, but it's how they mix them up that matters. You and your father may have some of the same genes, but you're not the same people.'

'But what if I've got the genes that made him ... act the way he did?'

'It doesn't work like that,' said Rick. 'People keep coming out with claims that they've discovered genes for violence and genes for intelligence and so on, but it just doesn't work like that. The genes are the raw materials, but we're all shaped by our environment as we grow up. We learn by experience, we learn to exercise self-control and judgement, we learn from those around us.'

And Danny had been brought up by a mass murderer. What lessons about life had he learned from his father, during all those years together? How had his father's influence moulded his own development in subtle ways, ways that no one would spot until maybe, that one day, when it would all be too late to change?

'Hey, look,' said Rick softly, nodding towards the swarm.

Bees were starting to peel away from the mass, buzzing around for a short time and then heading down to near ground level. A cluster of them were gathered on the hive's entrance block, and were starting to crawl inside.

'The ones we put into the old honeycomb have passed judgement,' said Rick. 'They've given the thumbs up, and now they're sending out scent signals to their swarm to tell them they've found a nice new home.'

More bees spiralled down to the hive, and Danny and Rick stepped back a short distance.

A few seconds later, a great block of bees split away from the mass, like ice calving from an iceberg. They descended on the hive, landing all over the front and on the grass at its base. Steadily, more and more bees came down, until the swarm had re-formed itself over the entrance to the hive.

As a demonstration of the relentless power of nature, it was impressive indeed.

9
Normal

He walked to school with Tim and Won't and sexy, sophisticated Jade – who seemed somehow just a little *less* beautiful this drizzly Monday morning. Little Rick had gone in David's ancient Mini today.

Danny walked in silence, his mind elsewhere.

There was no sign of Cassie and her friends from the other side of the village ahead of them on the track, or following behind, either.

That solved his immediate problem. How was he going to deal with her? How were they going to behave in front of everyone?

His little *Freundin*.

Or was she, even? His girlfriend. He didn't know.

They had kissed, but then she had turned that into one of her games: a fairy-tale kiss to break a spell.

They had held hands, but not for long.

Was he meant to do something? Make some kind of move? He had lived for so long by keeping everything in check, under control, but now this was a situation for which he didn't know the rules.

He had enjoyed being with her, but now it was as if

Saturday had happened to someone else. It was as if it had been someone else entirely who had relaxed with Cassie Lomax by the stream on the hill above Hope Springs. Someone else who had started to talk, to open up.

It wasn't the kind of thing Danny did. It broke all the rules he lived by.

'Hey, dreamer, I said see you later.'

He blinked. It was Jade. They were at school already. He nodded. 'Yes. See you later.'

He saw Cassie in maths, but she barely glanced in his direction. *She's playing it cool,* he thought. Or maybe she had been having second thoughts. There was, after all, no reason why she should be interested in him, not when she was sharing a desk with Scott Davies and Jase Lorrimer.

He wandered round at lunchtime deliberately not looking for her. If he had looked and not found her it would have been so much more disappointing than simply not looking in the first place.

A lane ran along the far side of the playing fields, and he followed this down to the river, past groups of smokers and a couple of older teenagers on motorbikes. Sand martins skimmed the surface of the river, darting up to holes in the far bank. Just above the holes an old woman walked a spaniel, unaware of the life beneath her feet.

A strange vibration jolted Danny out of his daydreams. His phone. He'd forgotten it was even turned on.

Val had bought it for him ages ago, to take with him when he and Oma went to visit his father. He hardly ever used it. He didn't have the kind of friends to make much use of it, really. He never let people that close.

He had swapped numbers with Cassie on Saturday, though.

He fumbled for it in his pocket. It had stopped vibrating. He pressed OK, then remembered the keypad was locked. By the time he had unlocked it he knew he had missed the call.

He stared at the small LCD screen. An envelope was blinking: he had a message.

He OK'd it.

Wlk hom 2gtha? C

He pressed OK to answer the message. What to say? Best to keep it simple.

Ok. Danny schmidt.

The surname thing was an afterthought, a shared secret. He hoped it would make her think of Saturday.

Moments after he had sent the message, she replied.

W8 by gates. CU L8R. C

He decided not to answer. It was clear enough. He would see her outside the main school gates after school.

The afternoon dragged.

She was there before him, leaning against a wall, her bag strap looped round her hand, bag on the ground. She gave him a quick smile. 'Hi, Schmidty,' she said. 'Going my way?'

They walked up Morses Lane, part of a steady flow of children tipping out of Severnside.

'What did you make of that maths homework?' Cassie asked.

'I haven't got a clue,' said Danny. 'It's all way over my head.'

'I thought as much. Want to come back to mine? You pick my brains if I can pick yours.'

'You can try if you like.'

They turned on to the track to Wishbourne.

Danny took out his phone. 'I'll let them know I'll be late,' he said.

Val answered.

'Hi,' he said. 'Me. I'm going to be late, okay? I'm going to a friend's to do homework.'

'Okay,' said Val. Then she added, 'That's good. I'll see you when you get in.'

'A friend, am I?' said Cassie.

'Could be worse,' said Danny. He realized he was grinning a stupid grin. He stopped himself, and looked down at the track. As he walked, he was aware of not just his own feet, but two more feet in the corner of his vision, walking faster to match his own long strides.

Cassie lived in one of the wooden chalets on Swiss Lane. From the way people talked of 'the other side of the village', he had always had the image of these houses as being little better than tumbledown allotment sheds, held together by string and paint.

Cassie's house was immaculate. The garden was neat and trim, everything geometric and evenly laid out. The house was painted a vibrant yellow, with white window frames – all so clean as if it had been painted only that day. A neat little silver saloon car was parked in the drive.

They went round to the back.

'Hi, Mum,' said Cassie, pulling the back door open and going into the kitchen.

Danny followed. Cassie's mother was a plump woman, probably in her early forties, with the same unruly black hair as her daughter. 'Hi, Cass,' she said. Then she looked up at Danny.

'This is Danny,' said Cassie quickly. 'I'm helping him with his homework. He's like, really sloooow.'

Her mother rolled her eyes at Danny. 'Tell me she's not like this at school, too,' she said.

'She's not. She's worse.'

'Not possible.' A man stood in the doorway, short and thin, a *Daily Mail* in his hands. 'Surely,' he added.

'Hi, Dad,' said Cassie, staring at Danny with narrowed eyes. 'You're home early.'

Out in the garden a few minutes later, they sat in the summer house, cans of Pepsi and their maths books spread out on a picnic table in front of them.

'So your dad's visiting, is he?' asked Danny. 'He doesn't *look* –'

'What? Bent as a nine-pound note?'

'You said your parents had split up.' She was staring down at her exercise book, but he knew she wasn't reading her work. He'd upset her. He'd messed things up.

'Okay,' she said softly. 'You found me out. My big dark secret. Every family has to have one, don't they? A skeleton in the cupboard. You know what mine is? My big secret that I try to hide? It's that *I'm* the ordinary, dull one. I'm an only child, with happily married parents, in a comfortable little picture-book cottage in a commuter village. Mum and Dad love me. We go on holiday every August, and every October half-term we stay with Nan in Prestatyn. It's such an ordinary life. And then . . . then I meet you and I'm like, how can I make myself seem interesting?'

She looked away again. After a few seconds, she said, 'Forgive me?'

He shrugged. She confused him all the time, whether she was telling the truth or not. It didn't make that much difference. 'Maybe,' he said.

'You can kiss me again later, if you want. Not now, though. Not here. Dad'd brain you. See him there in the window?' She waved at her father, who turned away instantly.

'I'll think about it,' said Danny.

'D'you believe in ghosts?' she asked, sparking off in a completely new direction in that way of hers.

'Hmm?'

'Life after death, that kind of thing.'

Rattled, he struggled for an answer.

'There's this cool website, that's all. Do you have a computer at home?'

'There's one I use,' he said.

'Cool. I'll text you later. So, what's yours?'

Another change of tack. 'My what?'

'Dark secret. Everyone has one, like I say.'

'You wouldn't want to know.'

'Go on,' she said, pushing him on the arm. 'Tell me what it is. Give me a clue.'

He shook his head. 'Really,' he said. 'You wouldn't want to know.'

Later, she walked with him from the house. At the top of Swiss Lane they came to the gap in the hedge where she had hidden from him last week. She stepped into the gap and he followed.

She reached up, pulled his head down, kissed him. Longer this time and, briefly, their teeth scraped together.

'I'll text you,' she said.

He left her in the hedge, and walked home, his head full of Cassie Lomax. Somehow, she had a way of breaking through all his carefully constructed barriers. He didn't know if that was a good thing or not.

Back at home, Val was red-eyed with recent tears.

She sat at the kitchen table with a glass of wine that was almost the same shade as her recently hennaed hair.

'Danny,' she said, brightening up as he came into the room. 'Did you get your work done?'

He nodded. 'What's up?' he said.

She hesitated, and then slid her newspaper across the table towards him. It was the *Echo*, folded open to the national news page.

He spotted the single paragraph instantly.

KILLER APPEALS

Anthony Smith, found guilty in 2001 of five murders, is to appeal against his conviction. Smith claims new evidence shows psychiatric reports used in his trial were misleading. His five mutilated victims, killed on a single night in April 2001, included Smith's aunt and a close friend. No date has been set for the hearing.

'It's all opening up again,' said Val, sloshing the wine briskly around her glass. 'I don't want to lose all this.' She flicked her head, indicating the flat, the Hall, Hope Springs, their new life, in that single gesture. 'I don't want us to have to go through all that again.'

'Nobody here knows,' said Danny. 'Smith's a common enough name. We'll be okay.'

As ever, it was Danny being calm, Danny taking control, Danny keeping things together. He always had to be the strong one.

10

Spirit Talk

Later, after they had eaten, Danny felt a vibration against his leg. He was in his room, in the window seat, looking out over the near-empty car park to where Sharmila and Luke and some of the others were helping a team put up the marquee on the lawn.

He took the phone out. He had a message.

Www.spirit-talking.co.uk CU there 2 chat? 6.30? C

He had ten minutes.

Ok. See you. D

He pulled his trainers on, and went out to the top of the stairs. He took the office key and headed down.

He let himself in through the front doors of Wishbourne Hall. The polished tiles, the grand sweep of a staircase before him and the high ceiling always made him feel that he had stepped into some kind of stately home.

There was a heavy wooden door to his right. He could see through the reception window that the office was empty. Although it was still sunny outside, the office itself was in gloom, with only a little light slipping in through the narrow leaded windows.

He turned the key in the lock and went inside. He

often came in here to do his homework. The computer was handy for printing, scanning and its Internet connection, but more than anything it was just . . . not the flat.

He pressed the power switch on the PC tower under the desk, and sat back in the swivel chair. No need to switch the light on. He looked around the office while the computer powered up.

A short time later, he typed 'www.spirit-talking.co.uk' into the address bar and pressed Enter.

The site was slow to load over the Trust's dial-up connection. A banner ad leaped into life first of all: 'GENUINE PSYCHIC READINGS! AS SEEN ON TV'. Below the banner, an ornate stone-effect frame was revealing itself, and a photograph of a smiling man who looked like a dentist. 'A big welcome to Spirit Talking, from your host, Dr Bob Walczinski,' it said under the smiling photograph.

While the page was still loading, Danny clicked on the Frequently Asked Questions link. 'What is a talk board?' the list of questions read. 'How do the talk boards work? Is it safe? Who are the spirit hosts? Can using the talk boards help you develop your psychic abilities? Can I have a talk board on my website? What kinds of questions can I ask? Can the spirit hosts predict my future?'

Danny checked his watch. He had a couple of minutes yet. He clicked on the first question, and it jumped down the page to where the question was repeated with a long paragraph of text below it. A talk board, according to the answer, was some kind of online cross between a Ouija board, tarot cards and a chat room. Log on to a talk board and you could talk directly to the inhabitants of the spirit world, and also to other people dumb enough to believe in all that garbage. That wasn't exactly how it described it in the FAQ, though . . .

He clicked Back, which returned him to the top of the page, and then clicked on 'Is it safe?'

It's important to stress here that talk boards aren't right for everyone (click here to arrange a consultation with one of our Qualified Practitioners). Approached with a Positive Attitude, our Boards are a good way for those new to Spirit Communication to get Involved. Remember: even if the Other Side does not call, our resident spirit hosts are there to interact with you so remember that your approach is vital – your Mental Energies set the tone. If your Energies are Negative you are sending an invitation to Bad or Mischievous Spirits. Any fears you have will be reflected right back at you if you are not careful. It is a good idea to visit our talk boards with an experienced friend at first (we also provide this service: click here for our Accompanied Chat option). So enter with Positivity and with a friend and we wish you well on your Spiritual Journey.
LEGAL NOTICE: spirit-talking.co.uk and its sponsors take no responsibility for this site's use or misuse or for any actions taken as a consequence.

Danny's phone buzzed against his thigh. Another message.

Whr RU?! C

He called her back.

'Where are you?' she said, straight away. 'I've been here for ages and I'm like, where is he?'

'This website . . . what is it? What are you doing there?'

'It's cool,' said Cassie. 'It's got loads of chat rooms – what it calls talk boards. Have you ever used a chat room?'

No. But before he could answer, she had moved on.

'So you can hang out with all kinds of people. But the cool thing is that even when you're alone there, the talk boards have what they call spirit hosts. They're like those smart characters built into games, programmed to give what seem like wise answers to anything you ask. They're a gas.'

'But why?'

'It's fun. That's why. And sometimes you can find out things about yourself, if you're up for it. It's the questions you ask that matter, not the answers. I know you're not into all this stuff – I've seen your looks! Just humour me, okay? It's somewhere we can get together and have a chat. And I mean *chat*, Danny Schmidt. It's no good giving me your mysterious silences when we're online. Do that in a chat room and you might as well not be there. You have to put something in.'

'Okay,' he said. He would humour her. She was trying to find ways to open him up, he realized. He still didn't understand why she would want to try. 'I'm there now,' he said. 'On the Frequently Asked Questions. What do I do?'

'Back to the home page, then "Talk Boards". I'm in number seven. Look out for the duckling.'

And she hung up.

He did as she said.

On the home page he paused. There was a big link in

the centre which urged him to pick today's card. He clicked and an image of a kind of playing card appeared on the screen. It was a picture card, showing a great wheel and what was presumably the Roman numeral, X. 'X. Wheel of Fortune,' the text below the card read. 'Make a wish and maybe you will be lucky.'

More superstitious nonsense. He clicked Back, and then followed the link to the talk boards.

It took him to a page where he was invited to sign in again, create a new login or enter as a guest. He chose the last option and was given the name Guest03. He chose 'Talk Board #7' from the list, and waited while the chat software kicked in.

It took him a few seconds to orientate himself. The main frame showed a list of the exchanges taking place in the room. According to the times listed, the last comment had been made three minutes ago: Dahlia telling Moondog that fools may well rush in but that means they get there first. Danny guessed that Dahlia must be one of the spirit hosts, and this one of its preprogrammed nuggets of wisdom.

At the foot of the screen, there was an input form where Danny could type in his own contributions to the chat room. And on the right there was a list of the room's occupants: Dahlia, Moondog, Duckling and Guest03. On the main screen it said:

Guest03 enters at 18:36BST

Dahlia says: Welcome, Guest03.

He typed a response, clicked Send and watched it appear on the screen.

Guest03 says: hello

Then he added:

Guest03 says: hi, ducklng

A pause, then a response.

Duckling says: RU from this side or th Other?

He realized his mistake. As he'd entered the chat room as a guest she didn't know who he was. Assuming, of course, that 'Duckling' was Cassie.

Then she followed up:

[Duckling says to Guest03: its U DS isnt it? C]

He looked more closely at the screen and saw that there was the option to reply to Duckling only, so no one else would see his response. He chose this and sent:

[Guest03 says to Duckling: it's me. DS]

FirstLady enters at 18:39BST

Dahlia says: Welcome, FirstLady.

On the right-hand side, he saw that there were now five of them in the room. He typed a message.

[Guest03 says to Duckling: how do u know if they're real people or spirit hosts?]

[Duckling says to Guest03: real ppl chose stpd namz like Guest03 ;-P]

[Duckling says to Guest03: U cant. U learn 2 spot em. They spell well!]

FirstLady says: What is this place?

Moondog says: 1st time here G03? (yr logins a giveaway)

Moondog says: NE1 here frm th utha side?

Dizzee enters at 18:41BST

Dahlia says: Welcome, Dizzee.

[Duckling says to Guest03: busy 2nite! look 4 nutha rm? jus u&i?]

Dahlia says: Does anyone have a question?

Moondog says: NE1 here frm th utha side?

Dizzee says: I have made the journey to be with you.

Moondog says: Nutha question.

FirstLady says: I think I am lost.

Moondog says: i thnk my grlz 2 timing. i need 2 no.

Danny sat back from the screen. His head was whirling with trying to keep up with the rapid exchange of messages. It was like talking to Cassie, only more so, he realized.

Outside, the sun had shifted behind the trees. The office was now submerged in a heavy gloom, so that the glare from the screen was dazzling when he looked back at it.

The flurry of messages had continued.

Near the top, he spotted a private one to him from Cassie. It was about to scroll off the screen – a few seconds later and he would have missed it.

[Duckling says to Guest03: i told u no moody silencs!! ask a q]

He thought.

Guest03 says: My card said to make a wish. What for?

FirstLady says: Hinzelmännchen? Is that you?

Moondog says: corny

Danny's head spun. He looked at the long list on the right. The virtual room had become crowded. Lots of conversations going on at the same time, all on the screen before him.

Headkin says: Wish for what you desire, but be prepared for the consequences.

FirstLady says: It has been long.

[Headkin says to Guest03: So what do you want, Danny?]

[Duckling says to Guest03: make a wish D – go on. i will 2.]

[Guest03 says to Headkin: I wish some things had never hapened. wish it could be liek before.]

Then he stopped. He stared at the screen. This 'Headkin' had been talking directly to him.

And he or she had used Danny's real name.

He looked at the times of the messages.

[Guest03 says to Duckling: What's going on?! What have you said to heakdin?]

At first he thought Cassie must have been playing games, but her message had been sent only a second after Headkin's so she couldn't have entered the chat room under two names and sent both.

Headkin says: Guest03 wants to change the past. Can't do that.

[Duckling says to Guest03: ???]

Moondog leaves at 18:47BST

[Guest03 says to Duckling: HK knows who I am! did u tell him my name?]

[Duckling says to Guest03: i sed zilch – u kidding me?]

FirstLady says: Make your wish, Danny. You can't change the past.

[Duckling says to Guest03: hey! 1st L did 2!]

Dahlia says: Does anyone have a question?

Guest03 says: Whats going on?

Dahlia says: Everyone sees a different slice of reality. The wise see more.

Headkin says: I can help you, Danny. We can do it together.

Guest03 says: This isn't funny. Im off.

[Duckling says to Guest03: whats happneing? D I don't like ths. What RU doing?]

FirstLady says: Stop teasing him, Hinzelmännchen.

Guest07 says: how duz this wrk?

[Headkin says to Guest03: You want things back to how they were, don't you, Danny? I can help you.]

FirstLady says: Poor boy. His daddy's locked away and his mummy's got a new boyfriend. We have to stop this, don't we? We have to make things how they were, don't we?

[Headkin says to Guest03: Let me help you. We can fix things together.]

Guest07 leaves at 18:52BST

[Duckling says to Guest03: answer me!!!]

'What's going on? What are you doing in here in the dark, Danny?'

Danny looked across at the doorway. Someone coming in. Short. Ponytail. It was hard to see as his eyes adjusted from the glare of the screen to the dim interior of the HoST office.

It was Little Rick.

'I . . .'

His hand felt locked in position, but he managed to shift it, move the mouse, click.

Guest03 leaves at 18:53BST

The screen paused for a few seconds with his farewell message, and then jumped back to the list of talk board options.

Little Rick had come to stand just behind Danny.

'So you're a secret chat-room addict, are you?'

Danny shook his head. 'First time,' he said. His mind was racing, struggling to grasp what had just happened. He looked at Rick, but could make out little in the gloom. He wondered how much he had been able to read before the screen changed.

'Occult stuff,' said Rick now, looking at the web page. 'I didn't know you were into all that crap.'

'I'm not.'

'Okay, okay. Whatever. Just don't let it get out of hand, okay? You need to be careful when you're doing this stuff.'

Rick left.

Danny shut down the computer. He sat in the darkness. He wanted to go and turn the light on. More than almost anything, he wanted that light on.

But he didn't dare move.

11

Opening Up

He was stirred into action by a buzzing against his leg.

The phone's LCD screen glowed in the murky room. Cassie's number.

'What are you playing at, Danny? What's going on? What was that all about?'

'I . . .'

'It's not funny. You freaked me out for a minute there. I don't know how –'

'Cassie.'

She stopped. She seemed to sense something in the tone of his voice. She waited for him to continue.

'Cassie, I don't know what happened in there. I'm not playing at anything.'

'Danny, he said your dad's locked up. Is that true? You're not just getting your own back because I made up stories about my own family?'

He hesitated. He had lost track of how much of the exchange with Headkin and FirstLady had been public and how much one-to-one.

'Can we talk?' he said.

He couldn't let this get out: the past, his father. It

would break Val if they had to go through all that again.

'We're talking right now.'

'Can you come out? It's not that late.'

'I might.'

'Top of Swiss Lane? Five minutes?'

She hung up.

She was late, but she came.

'I can't be long,' she said. 'I told them I was going to Jo's.' She looked back towards her house. 'Come on. I don't want to stop here.'

They headed back along the road into the older part of the village. At the bridge, they left the road and cut down the bank to a small cleared area in the undergrowth by the brook. This was one of the places where village kids came to smoke and make out.

Danny leaned back against the base of the bridge.

Cassie stood with her hands on her hips, peering at him in the twilight.

'So?' she said.

'I thought *you* might have some idea what happened. You've been to that chat room before. I haven't. I don't do that stuff.'

'It's never been like that,' she said. 'It's just a place to chat, and those weird spirit hosts spout words of wisdom every so often. It's usually funny. It's usually a gas. But this time . . . it really freaked me out, Danny. What was it?'

He'd never heard her like this. Uncertain, hesitant. Scared.

'They knew my name,' he told her. 'The one called

Headkin, he sent a message to me directly and called me "Danny". Then FirstLady did it, too.'

'I saw that one. Her message was open to everyone.' There was a silence and then Cassie continued, 'Okay. Be logical. When you signed in . . . I can't remember what you have to tell them when you sign in as a guest. Did you give your name or your e-mail or anything?'

He shook his head. 'Nothing. It just gave me that "Guest03" name and let me in. Nobody knew I was there, apart from you.'

'I wasn't doing anything,' she said sharply. 'I –'

'I know.'

'Maybe there was someone you know there. Maybe they worked out who you were somehow. I don't know. I don't understand.'

She moved towards him, and leaned with her head on his chest, his chin resting on the top of her head.

'I read some of the stuff about the site,' said Danny. 'The Frequently Asked Questions. It did warn about going in with a negative attitude. It said bad things could happen. Maybe they deliberately let it get weird sometimes, just to rattle people.'

'But they knew stuff, didn't they, Danny? That wasn't preprogrammed trickery. It was for real.'

He said nothing.

'I told you every family has to have a dark secret, didn't I?' said Cassie.

Silence, again. Danny had his eyes jammed tightly shut. When he opened them everything was blurred, slowly sharpening.

'One of them said your mum has a new boyfriend. Has she?'

'Maybe,' said Danny. 'I asked the guy the other day, but he didn't seem too certain. He calls round a lot. He'd like to be, I reckon. It's Little Rick – Mr Sullivan.'

'No! You're kidding me. But . . . well, teachers do it, too, I suppose. I mean . . . Mr *Sullivan*.'

He rubbed his chin against the top of her head. He could smell the shampoo on her hair.

'And your dad?'

'How did they know? Nobody knows that stuff.'

'I don't know,' she said softly. 'I'm freaked. I don't think I *want* to know.'

'Will you promise me something?' Danny said. He had his hands on her arms now, and he gently eased her away so that he was looking down into her face.

'Promise you what?'

'Don't talk about any of this – to anyone.' He realized now that he had to say more if he was going to persuade her. 'Mum had a really hard time with all this a few years ago. The trouble. She had to cope. That's why we came here: a fresh start in a place where nobody knows what we had to go through. Nobody judging us. We left all that behind. If it gets out here she'll be devastated.'

'You're not making sense, Danny. If *what* gets out?'

'The past.'

She was still looking up at him and he felt exposed. He pulled her towards him again, so that she was against his chest and he was looking over her. It was easier to talk like that.

'My father's in prison,' he said. They were words he had never spoken aloud before. 'He killed people.'

He felt her tense as soon as the words escaped his lips. This was all wrong, he realized. He was just going to turn her away from him. Quite rightly, too. Anybody in their right mind would run a mile from him.

'"People"?' she whispered. She had her hands up before her, against his chest; she pulled them tighter in, and then relaxed a little.

'He went mad one night,' said Danny. Not really *one night*. It had built up steadily: his father had watched Chris and Val, following them. Eva, too – he had hated her for some reason. Feared her. From what Danny had been able to make himself read of his father's journal, the madness seemed to have built over a period of a few weeks, until finally, one night, he had cracked.

'There was a big row. Dad was out somewhere. Mum wanted to go out to see a friend. She had an argument with Dad's Aunt Eva, and Eva went out instead.'

Danny had hidden upstairs in Oma Schmidt's room while his grandmother slept, which seemed to be all she did at that time. Eva was yelling at his mother: 'I come all this way because my family is calling to me. I come together with my family and what is it that I am finding? You! *Schlampe*, pulling the family apart. You cannot do it. I will not let you do it. Do you hear my words? You make Anthony like a fool. You see what you are doing to him? You drive a nail through his heart. You tell me where it is that you are meeting this man. You tell me now.'

Eva had gone. She went to tell his mother's friend that they were to stop meeting.

And so it was Eva who found his father at Chris Waller's house, kneeling over his best friend's body so that he could be in the best position to cut out his tongue. It was Eva who saw her nephew looking at her over the sights of her own old Luftwaffe Luger. That pistol must have been the last thing she had ever seen.

'He killed Eva,' Danny told Cassie now. 'And he killed a friend of his, who was also . . . a *friend* of my mother. And some others. Three. They were in the wrong place at the wrong time.'

'God.'

He had expected horror and Cassie was horrified.

He had expected shock and she was, clearly, shocked by what he told her.

He had expected revulsion, too, but no, far from being repelled by Danny and his story she was clinging to him more tightly, holding him.

'What must it have been *like* for you? God.' She pressed against him.

After a time, she asked, 'So . . . how did they know?'

For a moment he was thrown by her question.

'Your name,' she said. 'That your father is locked up and your mother might have a new boyfriend. How did they know those things in the talk board?'

'Someone from the past?' Danny said. 'Someone who's tracked us down and wants to stir everything up again?' But that still left a lot unexplained.

'Adam and Eve,' said Cassie slowly. 'Eve: the first

woman. FirstLady. Eve. Eva. She seemed lost. Confused. The talk board's supposed to be like a Ouija board, calling up spirits from the other side, talking to the dead.'

'Eva? No.'

'She said something that looked German.'

'Something *-männchen*,' said Danny. '"Little man"? What's that supposed to mean?'

'I don't know. That's what she was calling Headkin, though. She seemed to recognize him.'

That was when Danny saw it.

The connection.

All it took was hearing Cassie pronounce the name aloud.

Headkin.

'What?' She had sensed his body tensing. 'What is it?'

'I know that name,' he told her. 'Headkin. My father – he kept a journal. He wrote about the voices in his head that were driving him mad. He had a name for the voice that tormented him the most.'

'Headkin?'

'Almost. He called it Hodeken. The evil little man in his head. Taunting him. Driving him mad.'

'I'm scared.'

He held her tight.

Danny was scared too. More scared than he had ever been in his life.

12

Hodeken

Back at the flat, Josh was asleep and Oma Schmidt was cleaning the oven. 'Danny,' she said, when she saw him hanging up the office key. 'My boy. Is okay, *ja*?'

She seemed upset. Danny wondered if she had sensed his state of confusion and fear.

He nodded and Oma returned to her scrubbing, arms deep in the oven's interior.

'Where's Mum?'

Oma clicked her tongue in disapproval. 'He has been,' she said. 'Rick.'

So that was why she was upset. Danny wondered what Little Rick might have said. Had he come straight here from the office to tell Val that her son had been fooling with chat rooms and the paranormal?

He struggled to calm himself.

'They argued,' said Oma. 'I did not want to listen, but how to not? She went with him even so. Off together like the two loving birds.' She clicked her tongue again.

Danny suspected he knew the cause of their argument. Rick must have come here to tell Val that he had seen Danny logged on to a chat room. She would have been upset. She would probably have defended Danny. And now they would be discussing how to tackle his 'problem'.

He went to his room.

He slid the box out from under his bed and found the envelope.

Sitting in the window seat, he reminded himself why it was that he should always be in control of his own reactions. He reminded himself exactly what it was that he must never become.

And he listened.

In his head: silence. A thin whistling in one ear that he always had when he was stressed. The soft background sound of his breathing.

No voices, though. No evil spirits in his head, telling him what he must do.

Not yet.

It was after eleven when Val came home. Kicking-out time at the Wishbourne Inn – maybe that was where they had gone to debate Danny's failings.

He went out to the kitchen. Best to get any trouble over with as soon as possible.

She was at the sink, clutching a glass under the running cold tap. She turned. 'Danny,' she said. 'Okay?'

He nodded, and sat at the table.

Val drank, then stood with her hands on the edge of the draining board and sink, breathing deeply.

'Are *you* okay?' said Danny, uncertain how to interpret her mood.

She turned and stood, leaning against the sink edge with her arms wrapped round herself. 'Me? I'll survive,' she said.

'Oma said Rick was here.'

Val's embrace tightened. She nodded.

'I saw him earlier. In the Hall.'

'Oh?'

She didn't seem interested. They couldn't have discussed Rick finding Danny at the computer. Best to leave it, perhaps.

'Night.'

She looked at him, and nodded. 'Hmm,' she said. 'G'night.'

At lunchtime the next day, he was with Won't and Scott Davies and a couple of the others, down where the science building backed on to the playing fields. Won't and Davies were arguing about something. Danny wasn't sure what: it had started over football teams and had moved on to who was the sexiest girl in their history group. Won't never agreed with anybody on anything. That seemed to be a goal he set himself every day.

Danny tried to ignore them. His mind kept returning to the events of the previous evening. He couldn't make sense of it at all. He was even beginning to doubt that it had happened as he remembered – it all seemed so weird.

Someone batted him on the arm and he looked up, puzzled.

'I said, what about Mr Cool?' said Won't. 'What do *you* reckon, Danny?'

'About . . .?'

'Biggsy and Becky Taylor. I reckon they are. Davies says Biggsy's just daydreaming.'

Danny shrugged. 'Does it matter?'

'Hey, why d'you call him Mr Cool?' asked one of the others, someone Danny didn't know.

Won't said, 'You can say what you like to our Danny, but he won't lose it. Will you, Danny? He's Mr Cool. You'd have more chance with Becky Taylor than you would of rattling Mr Cool.'

Then he grinned, and added, 'Except, of course, when Cassie Lomax is around.'

Danny stared at him, but he didn't lose control. The sudden burst of rage he felt at Won't's digging and teasing never reached the surface. He sensed it, trapped it, squashed it.

He didn't lose his cool.

He didn't dare.

Won't was right. Cassie was the one person who got all the way through his barriers. She was the flaw in his defences, and suddenly that scared him. Things had started to go wrong since he'd got to know Cassie – since he'd let her weaken his guard.

Later, he left Won't and the others and headed for the top gate.

Cassie was there, with Jo Lee and Sally Gupta.

She looked pale and tired.

As soon as she saw him, she opened her mouth to speak, but then she must have sensed something about his mood and she stopped.

Sally and Jo laughed at something and Danny strode past, avoiding Cassie's look.

Not now.

He had to be alone.

Wlk hom 2gtha? C

He didn't answer, but she was waiting at the gates, even so.

'You okay?'

He nodded.

'You going to ask if I'm okay?'

He shrugged.

They walked. Danny heard Won't and Tim talking loudly somewhere behind them as they headed along Morses Lane. He glanced back, gave them the finger, carried on.

'You scared?'

'I don't know,' he told her. 'I don't know what I am.'

'So what have you found out?'

'What do you mean?'

'What are you *like*, Danny Schmidt?' She shook her head as she walked. 'You mean you haven't tried to find out what's happening? You've done *nothing*?'

She jerked her bag up by the strap and started to rummage through its contents. A short time later she waved a sheet of A4 at him. 'Here,' she said. 'Have a look at this. Have you ever heard of *kobolds*?'

Danny took the sheet. It was a printout of a web page.

THE KOBOLD

Kobolds are to be found in Germanic (Teutonic) folklore.

A kobold is a small, goblin-like, domestic spirit, who can be both helpful and mischievous. He often helps with household chores, but sometimes hides tools and implements. He can get very angry if he is not fed properly. The kobold can be an unpredictable creature, dangerous when crossed, and fiercely protective of the family in his care.

Some kobolds are believed to be spirits dwelling in caves and mines. Other kobolds have specific names – like Goldemar or Hodeken. Goldemar can see the secret sins of the clergy, while Hodeken taunts unfaithful wives.

'You're telling me we have a family gremlin?'

'You're the one who talked about inner demons,' said Cassie. She snatched the paper back and shoved it into her bag.

'In my father's head,' said Danny. 'He was mad. Hearing voices.'

'Hodeken's voice, you said.'

He nodded. 'Maybe he knew the kobold legend,' he said. 'Maybe it was in a story he was told when he was a child, and when he started to crack up it came back to him: the name, the memory of an angry little spirit.'

'This is like *Scooby Doo*,' said Cassie.

He looked at her, waited for her to explain.

'In every episode something freaky happens, but they always end up finding a perfectly rational explanation for it all. It's usually the janitor.'

'It's better than not having an explanation.'

'But what about the talk board?' Cassie reminded him. 'How do you explain that?'

He couldn't.

'Okay,' he said. 'Let's go with the Hodeken thing. Some kind of domestic demon that's attached to our family, causing all our problems. A German curse. So where is it? Where is it hiding? Why haven't we seen it?'

'It's spoken to *you*,' said Cassie softly, reacting to his raised voice. 'On the talk board. Some people say they're all around us – spirits, ghosts, strange entities – but most of us are just too blind to see anything out of the ordinary. We've all forgotten how to see them.'

'You believe that?'

'I don't dismiss it,' she said, still talking softly. 'Maybe you just need to learn to look properly.'

He shook his head. He was worked up and he fought to calm himself.

'Maybe it's me,' she said hesitantly.

'What?'

'Maybe *I'm* the kobold. The mischievous spirit that's entered your life. You have to think the unexpected.'

He remembered his earlier realization that Cassie was the one person who could get under his defences.

He shook his head again, angry and confused. 'I don't need this,' he muttered. She was playing mind games with him, stirring up things best left untouched.

Silence. They were near the end of the track now.

'I can't work you out, Danny Schmidt.'

He looked at her, puzzled.

'I don't know how to read you. You're so aloof all the

time, as if you're above little things like being friendly and talking to people. Talking to me. You hold the world at arm's length. And then sometimes I think I'm connecting. But I'm not. I don't think I've ever connected with you, have I?'

He watched her as she spoke.

He kept himself calm, in control again.

'I can't even begin to imagine what it's been like for you, to have been through what you've been through,' she continued. 'But I'm trying. I don't know what's happening now, either. You have problems, Danny. You've come up against something really ancient and frightening and if you don't handle it just right your world will explode.'

'No,' he said. He couldn't believe what she was telling him.

The battle he had to face was the battle he had been facing for the last three years: the battle not to lose to the family madness, not to end up like his father. That was what it came down to.

And the way to do that was to shut everything – and everyone – out.

Cassie was watching him.

'You know where I am,' she said. And she turned, and headed off towards Swiss Lane. Soon the curve of the road had taken her from his sight.

13

Berlin, August 1961

He wandered around the empty flat. Shortly after they moved in, David had told him that when Wishbourne Hall had still been a school, this was the sick bay. Sometimes, Danny thought he could still detect that antiseptic medicinal odour, as if it were imprinted on the walls. Now, the flat's main smell was a mixture of polish and the dahl soup Val had been preparing for their evening meal.

Domestic sprites. Spirits of the caves and mines. Spring sunshine poured into the flat. There were very few dark corners in which a kobold might hide. It was the stuff of children's stories: enchanted cottages in the woods, mysterious castles and wicked stepmothers. These things just didn't fit into a modern flat like this.

He thought back to their house in Loughton, around the time when everything had been turned upside down. It was an ordinary, 1930s semi-detached house, with a small, trim front garden, a drive at the side and a long back garden.

It hadn't been occupied by any supernatural being. It

hadn't been haunted by a legendary creature from his family's German past.

He would have known. He was sure he would have known that something was amiss.

Most people are blind to them, Cassie had said. We've forgotten how to see them.

'Anybody there?' he called softly.

Nothing.

He walked around again. Just a flat. An ordinary flat.

That night he lay on his back in bed. The curtains were open, the frosty blue light of the stars and the half-moon casting the room in shadows.

He listened, but there was nothing. No sounds in the room or the flat. No sounds in his head.

No voices.

Lots of dark hiding places at night. Places where a creature of the caves and mines might feel at home.

Everything seemed different in darkness.

Under his bed: the box, the envelope of memories . . . what else? His wardrobe stood against the far wall, one door not quite closed.

He reached for the lamp and turned it on, blinking at the sudden light.

It was like being a small boy again. Night terrors.

He climbed out of bed and walked around his room.

He leaned on the wardrobe door to close it, then opened it immediately – just shirts, trousers, blazer, shoes – and then pressed it closed once again.

Under the bed. The box. His trainers. A tissue and some socks. A pile of board games. A couple of bags.

Back in bed, Danny slept as soon as his head hit the pillow. It was as if a spell had been cast upon him: lie down and you shall sleep.

And when you sleep you shall dream . . .

He looked at himself reflected in the dark glass of the window. He stared into his own dark eyes and then he realized that the person in the glass was different. He was looking at a woman – a young woman. Great-Aunt Eva, looking at herself in the glass.

This was Eva's story.

She had been disturbed from a light sleep by unfamiliar noises from outside. Now, at the window, she peered out but nothing seemed to have changed.

She did not know what time it was, but it must be late. She had been out to the American sector of West Berlin tonight with Walter and her older sister, Konstanz. She would marry Walter one day. She had decided this at one point this evening when she and her sister had been drinking fizzy wine and smoking his cigarettes.

A lorry rumbled past below, laden with coils of barbed wire and fence posts. That was unusual, but soon it was gone.

And then . . . the sound of a distant pneumatic drill. It was this that had woken her.

She went to the mantelpiece and found the delicate little watch that Walter had given her on her birthday two months before.

It was nearly two o'clock in the morning. She went back to bed just as another lorry rumbled by below.

In the morning, Eva picked up the news from a radio tuned to RIAS in the West. The border between East and West Berlin had been closed overnight. Barbed wire divided the two halves of their city, and it was only possible to cross at certain points, and even then only if one had all the right papers.

Eva sat and listened in shock. Her brothers, Christian and Dieter, had been in the West last night, working late on a construction site and then sleeping over as they sometimes did. Konstanz's husband, Bernhard, had been out on military exercises with their Factory Fighting Group. And Walter – had he made it safely home? Whatever would become of them all?

Somewhere in the back of her mind, Eva sensed a stirring, a small presence lurking. A voice, whose words she could not, as yet, make out.

She woke Konstanz and told her the news.

'I am going out to see,' she said. 'I think you should rest here.' Konstanz was pregnant and Eva was concerned about her health, but already her sister was out of her bed and pulling on some clothes.

It was early, barely eight o'clock on a Sunday, and yet there were people out on the streets. Most looked blank and few were even talking. All headed towards the border. Eva and Konstanz followed the drift of people.

'Look!' Konstanz gestured down Charlotten Strasse, and they paused, and then turned down the side street. A small crowd had gathered where the street was crossed by Zimmer Strasse. This junction marked the boundary between the sectors, and now an evenly spaced row of men stood across it, machine guns held tensely across their chests. Behind them, more men uncoiled barbed wire from great rolls, stringing it up across concrete posts that had been newly planted in the road.

That explained the drilling sounds overnight: they had been making holes for the fence posts.

'My God,' said Konstanz softly. 'The Factory Fighters . . .'

Of course. It suddenly made sense: the 'military exercises' of last night had been nothing of the sort. The Factory Fighter Groups had been the ones who were dividing their own city with wire while their fellow Berliners slept.

The rest of the day passed in a blur.

The two sisters moved from point to point along the new barrier. They spent much of the time standing in crowds, just staring through the wire at the other side. Crowds in the west of the city did likewise, so that the workers were watched from both sides as they unravelled their wire in silence. Occasionally, someone on one side or the other jumped and waved and called a name, and sometimes received a response from the other side. Some pleaded with the border guards to be allowed through, but the guards simply shook their heads. Nobody was to pass.

They rested outside Friedrichstrasse Station. Eva felt dizzy. She felt a great pressure inside her head.

They had learned here that the few local trains between East and West would run from Platform B, where the police would only allow entry to those with official permission to travel. Their return from the dance last night must have been one of the last normal services to have run.

All around them, Eva sensed a net closing. The barriers were shutting out the corrupt West, but also it was shutting them in, confining them.

She knew whose voice it was in the back of her head.

'What do we do now?' asked Konstanz weakly.

'Ask the *Hinzelmännchen*,' said Eva. 'We should ask Hodeken for guidance. He has helped us before. He senses our need now. I can feel it. We should ask him to guide us again.'

Monday and Tuesday were strange.

It was as if the whole thing had been carefully timed so that it would work out just this way. Give people all of Sunday to get used to the change and then on Monday . . . back to work as normal.

For most people, at any rate. Konstanz went down to the hairdresser on Muhlenstrasse to wash and set hair, and hope that her Bernhard was okay. But Eva . . . Eva was a *Grenzgängerin*: someone who, until this day, had lived in the East and worked in a restaurant in the West.

So Eva was at a loose end. She walked until she was exhausted but everywhere it was the same: nowhere to cross, the city well and truly split in two.

It still did not seem possible. *It has happened*, the voice told her. *You must act.*

But how?

At one point on the Tuesday, Eva was in a small crowd near the Church of Reconciliation on Bernauer Strasse. The border ran right along the front of the buildings here and the road itself was in West Berlin, out of reach. Wire was strung across the end of each of the side streets, guarded by Factory Fighters, all watched by staring Westerners from the far side.

One old woman turned to Eva and said, 'I can go in her back door and step out the front and I'll be in the West.'

Another, younger, woman leaned towards her and said, 'Mother! Do not say these things.' She glanced at Eva. 'You do not know who will hear.'

Berliners scared of each other. Scared that anyone might be an informer. That was how it had become.

Eva turned away, but even as she did so, her mind was racing. She could do that, too. She could just go up and knock on a door and find someone who would let her walk through to the West.

No. Think of the family. You must not act selfishly, alone. She calmed herself, thankful for the small voice in the back of her head. She loved her faithful *Hinzelmännchen*. He had given them so much.

Eva headed north. She paused on Ruppiner Strasse early in the afternoon. Where the street joined Bernauer Strasse she saw a truck, and men unloading it. A stack of concrete building blocks stood by the back of the truck.

They are building a wall.

Eva's first reaction to the division of Berlin had been that this must be a short-term measure, a defiant gesture aimed at the West. But now . . . they were bricking up the end of this street, and no doubt other streets right across the city. This had the look of permanence.

She thought again of the women at Bernauerstrasse, where it was possible to enter a house's back door in the East and walk through its front door into the West.

She turned, and headed back across Mitte district towards the apartment. Hodeken, her little voice, had been right. *Think of the family. You must not act selfishly, alone.*

That had always been their way, and it would be so now.

She kept quiet about it, at first.

She knew they must leave, but also, she knew that Konstanz's husband, Bernhard, believed that what had happened was a good thing: the erection of the Wall was a defining moment in their nation's short history.

Late at night, Eva stood alone, staring out of the window of the room she shared with Konstanz and Bernhard. 'Tell me I am right,' she said softly.

Hodeken nodded. *You are right, Eva. You know that you are. Things will get worse here. Germans will shoot Germans because of this thing.*

'But what do I do?'

Be patient. I am looking after you.

'You have been quiet, little one. I thought we had lost you.'

I have not been needed. I have been resting. I will always be here in your time of need.

★

That evening, Eva and Konstanz sat in a bar a few minutes from the apartment. They sat at a small circular table, smoking and drinking weak coffee.

'We have to leave,' Eva urged her sister. 'But we must be cautious. We must wait and learn. We must work out the best way to do it and then we cross the border into the West and find Christian and Dieter.'

That was what Hodeken had told her they should do. Spur of the moment escapes had worked to start with, but they would be less and less likely to succeed. They needed to plan carefully to reunite the family.

'But how would we survive there?' asked Konstanz.

'We survived the war,' said Eva. 'We survived the early years when the Soviet army first occupied our land.'

'We had help,' said Konstanz.

Eva nodded. 'We have help again. The *Hinzelmännchen* has awoken. Hodeken has sensed our need.'

In a small voice, Konstanz said, 'I cannot go.'

Eva stared at her.

'Bernhard,' Konstanz said. 'He would not want to run. I cannot go without him.'

And Walter, Eva suddenly thought. They had seen each other only briefly over the last few days, and today she had not given him a single thought until now. Would he join them? And what would she do if he refused?

'We have time yet,' Eva said. 'The family will not be divided.'

Konstanz's husband would have nothing to do with the proposed escape until late the following week when the first person was shot, trying to escape across the

Humboldt Canal. 'I could not do such a thing,' he said, several times that evening. 'I could not shoot my neighbour.'

'But you might be ordered to,' Eva told him.

'I know.'

So it was that the two sisters, Eva and Konstanz, shut themselves in a small room in the apartment that they shared.

'Hodeken,' said Eva, softly. 'We need you, little one.'

She glanced at the window, and she saw the little man reflected in the glass.

She turned, and he was there, perched on the edge of Konstanz's mattress, bony knees tucked up under his chin and a conical grey felt cap pulled down hard on his head. He looked at them one by one. 'Only two,' he said. 'I leave you alone for a time and what do you do? You lose your brothers in the West. So what is it you wish for? You want me to make everything all right again, is that it?'

He was grinning, his yellowed teeth glistening from his leathery old face. Hodeken was happy. He was in his element. He was going to solve all their problems.

'You see, Danny?' He turned away from the two, who leaned close together, talking and plotting. He was looking at Danny, who was in the room now, sitting on the mattress by the little man's side.

'You see, Danny?' he said again. 'This is how it has been and how it should be. The family, pulling together. Sometimes the family needs help, though. Sometimes they need their *Hinzelmännchen*.'

Hodeken straightened proudly. 'I am a legend. You know? You are honoured.' He chuckled. 'I helped them get through the war, and then I helped them survive the coming of the Soviet soldiers, which I tell you was harder than surviving the war in many ways. And now . . . now they need me again, and so I help them with their plotting and their planning.' He nodded towards the two, still deep in conversation.

'What do you want? What do you want with me?' asked Danny.

'I want what you want,' said Hodeken. 'You told me, remember? You want things how they were. You want your family to be normal again. That's a tough one, but I'm a legend, aren't I?'

'It's not possible.'

'Not while your mother behaves as she does,' said Hodeken. 'How can the family be whole again while your mother goes off with another man? She did it before, and look what happened. Trust me, Danny. Together we will fix everything and you will have your wish.'

'No,' said Danny. Wishing something had never happened was different to wishing to go back.

'Trust me, Danny. You will have your wish.'

'No. Look what happened to Dad . . .'

Hodeken smiled. 'Your father didn't trust me, Danny. I scared him. Do I scare you, Danny? Are you as weak as your father? He didn't understand. I want you to understand so that we can work together and make the family strong again. If you do not trust me . . .' Hodeken shrugged. 'I cannot help it but things may go wrong.'

'What happened in Berlin?' Danny asked, a thought suddenly occurring to him. 'What happened to Eva?'

A shrug. 'That's not what I'm here to show you.'

'Why? What happened to her?' She had not left Berlin until much later – they had even thought she must be dead until she eventually made it to the West.

Hodeken looked cornered. He said nothing.

'What happened?' Danny demanded, a final time.

They sat in the kitchen and drank coffee. Eva leaned forward and took Walter's hand across the table. 'Will you come with me, Walter my love? There is no future here. I want to be in the West with my sister and brothers. I want to be with you.'

Walter looked puzzled. 'But Konstanz is here, not in the West, is she not? I do not understand.'

'Tomorrow night,' said Eva. 'She and Bernhard will be in the West. *I* will be in the West. Come with me, Walter. Marry me and start a new life in another country with me.'

She didn't dare look at him. Walter was a very proper man, a gentleman, and she loved him dearly. She did not think he would come with her. Hodeken had even told her not to ask. *Say nothing. He will not come, so why tell more people than you must?*

Walter surprised her. Her proposal had thrown him. 'Let me consider,' he told her finally. 'Let me think what to do.'

'Later,' she said, and kissed him.

*

The following night, four of them gathered on Wilhelmstrasse, a short walk from the Wall. Eva, Konstanz and her husband Bernhard, and, finally, Walter, looking paler and more scared than any of the others.

Eva hugged him.

'I . . .' He gestured at his bad leg, an old war wound. 'I do not wish to be a burden. It is some time since I could claim to be a man of action.'

'You're no burden,' said Eva.

They followed an alleyway and minutes later they saw the River Spree through the wire. The Factory Fighters had strung barbed wire across the end of this alleyway, leaving an open promenade by the river clear, a no-man's-land.

Bernhard cut the lower strands of wire with a pair of cutters and carefully peeled them back.

They crawled through and then scurried across the open area to the shelter of a tree. There they began to strip off their clothes, down to their underwear.

All the time, Eva was aware of a small figure sitting on the wall by the river, face hidden in the shadow of his felt hat.

She turned, and saw that Walter had only removed his coat. He was grimacing.

'My knee,' he said. 'I strained it under the wire.'

'You will be okay,' said Eva, more an instruction than a question. 'We swim together. I will help you.'

'Yes, yes.'

Already, the other two were on the wall, ready to drop into the dark waters of the Spree.

Go on! You have little time, my children. Leave him, Eva, go!

She couldn't. She helped Walter with his jacket.

She heard the soft splashes as the others entered the water.

Walter took her arm. He had her top in his other hand. 'Put this on,' he said. 'Go back. There is still time.'

That was when she began to understand Hodeken's warning.

You could trust no one these days. Anybody might turn out to be an informer, telling stories to the people's police, or worse, to the state security police, the Stasi.

Anybody.

She took her top – she had to, he thrust it right at her – and backed away, feeling as if her world had been dragged out from under her feet.

She reached the low stone wall, but it was too dark to see anyone in the water.

She looked across, and Walter had produced a pistol, a Luger, and he was aiming down into the water.

She kicked out at him, the man she had loved. She struck him on his injured knee and his leg buckled. His hands swung upwards, and a shot went high into the air. The flash from the gun's muzzle surprised her almost as much as the sudden noise, so close to her head.

That must have been the signal, the first shot. A floodlight came on, shining down from the bridge, and its beam swung across the water.

Someone shouted a warning, and a shot was fired. Then another. Another.

The floodlight was suddenly extinguished and the firing halted.

Blinking, Eva peered up at the bridge, and there she saw a tiny figure skipping along the parapet.

Hodeken!

There was more shouting up there now.

She turned and looked down, wondering now why Walter had gone quiet.

He was dead.

A stray bullet must have struck him. A ricochet.

Go. Too late to swim now.

She ducked down and took Walter's gun, and then, clutching her clothes to her chest, she ran for the gap they had cut in the wire.

'They didn't do what I said, Danny. I *told* Eva not to tell Walter.'

They were in the Berlin apartment again, Eva moving around in a trance, packing the things she would need. She was not going to stay here for much longer. It was too risky, now that the rest of her family had fled.

'It is futile,' said Hodeken, shrugging. 'The Stasi will come for her and arrest her and this time there will be nothing I can do. There are some things in this modern world that are hard for an ancient being like me to deal with . . .

'The *Neues Deutschland* only reported one death: Bernhard Schmidt, Konstanz's husband. Shot in the water and pulled out the next day. Your grandfather, Danny. I am so sorry, but what could I do?'

'You failed them,' said Danny. 'You got it wrong.'

Hodeken shook his head sadly. 'If only little Eva

had done as I told her. Everything would have worked out. You just need to trust me, Danny, and everything will be fine.

'Konstanz found her brothers, Christian and Dieter, in West Berlin and, eventually, when they had given up hope for Eva, they left for a new life in England.

'Poor Eva. On her own now, in a city that has become a different city. She does not know what has happened. While she is in prison, she will vow to reunite the family, and I will promise to help her. But it is hard, and it is a long time before I get her out of jail. And by then it is a struggle simply to survive, as she hears no news of her brothers and sister . . . She will cope. She will survive. And when Eva finally finds her family again, I know I will be needed and so I travel with her, all the way from Berlin.'

Hodeken turned, and gazed at Eva as she packed.

Danny watched her, too.

When she had finished, she slid down with her back against the wall, and sobbed. Hodeken went to her, put his arms round her, and the two embraced.

Finally, Hodeken looked up and winked. 'Trust me, Danny. Trust me and you will get your wish.'

Danny blinked, and when he looked again, Eva was alone, hugging herself tightly. From beyond the room, there was a heavy knock at the door. She reached to her belt for the pistol, but Hodeken shook his head and took it from her gently. A heavy weight crashed against the door and it splintered on its hinges.

★

When he woke, there was a pressure on his chest, a gentle weight. Something pressing softly down.

He felt the panic rising.

Half awake, he swung an arm.

And struck something. A figure, a creature. A being.

He opened his eyes, but it was dark.

He brought both arms up again, but this time there was nothing.

He pressed at his chest, clawing at himself as if trying to peel the T-shirt from his body.

He fumbled for his lamp, fearfully, not wanting to reach out from his bed, thinking at any moment that some nightmarish creature might grab his wrist.

The light came on, momentarily blinding him.

He peered around the room, but there was nothing. No thing. Nobody.

He turned on to his side and curled up into a tight ball.

Out in the kitchen, Oma was still moving about. She was humming softly, and now the sound drifted into Danny's room, calming him, soothing him. She had done this when he was little, singing for him, calming him when he had woken with the night terrors.

He closed his eyes tightly and longed for morning.

14
Voices . . .

In his head. Echoing around inside his skull as he lay awake the next morning. Eva sobbing, alone in the empty Berlin apartment. Konstanz, giggling over a glass of sparkling wine the night before Berlin was split in two. All four of them, talking nervously on the night of their attempt to swim across the River Spree, a night on which two of them were to die and one would be stranded, lost, and finally arrested for aiding those violating border regulations.

And Hodeken, of course. The *Hinzelmännchen*. Their family guardian.

Their family *madness*, now lodged deep in Danny's head.

Trust me, Danny. Trust me and you will have your wish. Together we will fix everything and your family will be as it was, and as it should be.

He couldn't get that nasal little voice out of his head, no matter how hard he tried.

He took his phone out, and looked in the names under 'C'.

Only one entry there.

Cassie knew stuff. She understood, despite her kooky, off-centre approach to things.

But he was frightened she would turn him away. He didn't think she wanted to have anything to do with him any more, after they had argued on the way home from school. *He* wouldn't, if he were her.

Trust me.

He walked to school. He was with the usual group from Hope Springs. Or rather, he wasn't really walking *with* them. He was walking in the same direction, at the same speed, but he wasn't taking part.

He was walking to school alone, shutting the others out.

Cassie was ahead, with Jo Lee and a couple of the other Wishbourne girls. She didn't look back a single time.

Danny was exhausted, as if he had not slept at all the previous night. He wanted to share it all with Cassie, to unburden himself, but he knew he could not. He had to keep it to himself.

'Val tells me you're going visiting again on Saturday,' said Rick, at Danny's side.

Danny glanced down at him. 'That's right,' he said.

'Must be tough,' Rick said.

'It's how it is,' said Danny. Mr Cool, keeping the world at arm's length. Walking to school alone, in a crowd.

'Do you like it here?'

Thursday evening, and Danny and Val were working one of the vegetable plots, hoeing carefully between the rows of onions in their raised beds. Josh was in one of the empty beds, digging with a spare trowel he seemed to have found from nowhere. Danny had paused to watch him, drawn to the little fellow's obsessive digging. He had excavated quite an impressive burrow in the rich soil.

Danny looked around at the lake glistening through the trees, the Hall beyond the plots, the hill beyond that. Until recently, it had been a peaceful place. They had settled into a way of life, a way of moving on from tragedy.

'Like' wasn't a word he would have chosen, though.

'We're doing well,' he said in reply. 'It was a good move.'

'Good,' said Val. 'We can make it work, can't we?'

'Why are you asking?'

She hugged herself. 'I need reassuring,' she said. 'Sometimes I need to be told that things are okay. Do you know what I mean?'

'Maybe you should come with us to see Dad,' he said, watching her carefully. She looked away instantly. 'See how he's changed. He seems . . . stable. We've all made progress.'

She shook her head. 'I'm not on the Visiting Order,' she said. 'It's just you and Oma. Someone has to stay here and look after Josh.'

Excuses. They both knew she was simply making excuses. She could always be put on the V.O. next time. She was avoiding the issue, as she always did.

'You could divorce him.'

'No.' An instant answer, no need to consider.

'Why?' Why not make a completely clean break? He had never dared press her on any of this before.

She looked at him now. 'Because it scares me,' she said, finally. After another pause, she continued, 'I don't want to push too hard. I don't want any of the old weirdness to come back into our lives.'

Danny swallowed. He had to deal with this himself. He couldn't confirm her fears.

'Dad's in prison. He can't do anything.'

She tipped her head to one side, shifting her gaze to somewhere in the distance.

'I know,' she said. She didn't seem convinced that was enough, though.

She forced a smile. 'I'm glad you're happy here, Danny. We'll make it work, won't we?'

Danny sat with Oma Schmidt in the Visitors' Centre. Children were all around them, laughing and playing and fighting, and tired-looking mothers yelled at them or ignored them altogether.

As usual, Oma was happy. She sat in her plastic seat, rocking back and forth, humming a little tune with a smile on her face.

She was going to see her little boy, and all was right with the world.

She had another photograph with her. It showed Danny with his father and one of the German great-uncles on a beach somewhere. Danny was wearing a nappy that sagged to knee level. His father was supporting him by the hands, and to the side, the uncle stood with his trousers rolled up to mid-calf, ankle-deep in the sea yet still wearing a tie and jacket.

'I wonder where they are now,' said Danny. He meant Dieter and Christian, Oma's two brothers.

'They were scared,' said Oma. 'But they will be back. Many years ago we made a promise to each other. We would support each other. Brothers and sisters. Family. Fifty, sixty years ago – we went through much, but we survived. Is good now. Your father, he is having his appeal. After that, my Christian and Dieter will remember their duty to the family.'

Danny said nothing.

Soon, their number was called and they went through to be searched and scanned, and finally to be allowed in to the visiting hall.

The faces greeted them, and then all but one turned away again, disappointed.

His father looked at them blankly, without the usual uncertain smile, or the wave to come over and join him at his table, in case, for some reason, they might otherwise decide to sit elsewhere.

They went and sat.

He didn't reach out and take Oma's hand. He didn't say anything.

Danny felt dizzy. As if he were tumbling headlong down a funnel into the past. His father . . . this man sitting across the table seemed like an empty shell of the man he had expected.

Oma Schmidt was not her usual prison-visiting self, either. She seemed to sense that something was not quite right. There was no smile in her eyes, no air of contentment simply to be with her son once again. She had the photograph in her hand. She reached forward and placed it on the table, smoothing it with her fingers as if it might otherwise curl up into a ball.

Danny's father looked at her, and then down at the picture.

'How's the appeal?' asked Danny. 'What's happening with that?'

Now, his father's eyes lifted slowly. Still, he had said nothing.

'Your appeal. The journal. Mr Peters,' said Danny, struggling to find the switch that would flick his father back to normality.

'I thought I'd stopped it.'

His father's voice was flat, as if every word was a struggle.

'What? The appeal? You've stopped it?'

His father shook his head, briefly. A single movement. He raised a hand to his temple and pressed – so hard that Danny could see the tendons and veins standing out on the back of his hand.

'I had their tongues. I shut them up.'

Danny stared at him.

'I thought I'd stopped them.' His hand was still pressing. 'The voices,' he added. 'Stopped . . .'

Danny didn't want to be here. Didn't want to be listening to these words or seeing his father like this.

He wasn't here for this. He was here to . . . to move *on*, not back.

His father spoke again, but the words came out in a rush, a guttural eruption of something that sounded German and yet was either too fast or too distorted for Danny to make out. And he spoke those words in a voice that was different: higher-pitched, more nasal, as if he was pinching his nose as he spoke. More penetrating.

Danny wanted to look away, but he could not. He was transfixed.

He stared at his father's eyes, but they were not his father's eyes. They were pale, the irises tiny black pin-pricks, the whites netted with red blood vessels. The skin around his eyes was darker, more leathery, broken by lines and warts.

He felt that he was falling, and yet he knew he had not moved from his chair.

He stared into Hodeken's face.

'It is all right,' the nasal little voice said to him, soothing him, smothering the panic that had been bubbling to the surface. 'It will not be long now. It is all okay.'

Danny felt calm now. He managed to smile. All okay.

'Hey, I remember that.'

It was his father again. He still had the hand on his temple, but now he had spotted the photograph. He smiled, nervously. 'Eastbourne, wasn't it?' He rubbed at his head, then lowered his hand.

Oma smiled at him. She always managed to bring something that would get through to her son.

Danny sat back in his chair. He felt dizzy. He did not know what it was that he had just experienced.

He put a hand to his temple and pressed hard.

Nothing.

He lowered his hand, pleased that Oma and his father seemed happy. Whatever it was . . . it didn't matter now.

15
Talking

'Who is Hodeken?'

Oma looked up at Danny, eyebrows raised. 'Is a funny question,' she said, and then returned to the washing up.

Danny took another plate to dry.

'It was the name in Dad's journal,' he said. 'I expect it'll come up in his appeal.' He watched her reactions closely, wondering how much she might reveal about the family's past, how much of it might even be true.

'It means "Little Hat",' she told him, a distant look in her eyes. 'Is a *Hinzelmännchen*, a household spirit from the old tales. A legend. Like Hansel and Gretel, Rumplestiltskin and Snow White, yes?'

'Fairy tales,' said Danny.

'The tales are not to be dismissed,' she said. 'Is much truth in the old tales. Your Great-Aunt Eva always loved Hodeken. Is the only story she remembered our mother telling to her. Hodeken, he lived with the bishop of Hildesheim and the two of them, they had good times together and they helped each other greatly. Hodeken is a practical joker and he brings laughter to the life of the bishop. But then they had a falling out and the bishop banished Hodeken who was left to make a life wherever he could. After that neither of them were happy again for a long, long time.'

'And what is the truth in *that* old tale?'

Oma laughed, and flicked some foam at Danny. 'The truth there is that you should listen to us old ones. If you go against the old ways like the bishop and you ignore the old wisdom, too, you will not be happy for a long, long time!'

He wanted to ask her if she believed in Hodeken, if what he had seen in his dream was the truth.

But he couldn't. How to ask such a question? On this sunny afternoon, it didn't seem like a thing he could ask without looking stupid.

And maybe, just a little, the answer frightened him.

Cassie would be able to suggest something. She had ideas and insight, where it was all Danny could do just to get by.

But he couldn't ask her.

She would look things up, he knew. Investigate. He could do that just as well.

He went to the office and let himself in with Val's key. This was the first time he had been here since he and Cassie had been spooked by the spirit hosts on that talk board.

That was the first time Hodeken had spoken to him. Voices on the screen instead of voices in his head or in his dreams.

He did a search on the Berlin Wall. It had gone up

in the early hours of Sunday 13 August, 1961: first the barbed wire, and then a couple of days later, the bricks.

He looked for Hodeken, and found the page that Cassie had printed for him. Following another link, he found that kobolds were very devoted, and would become attached to a particular place or family. A chosen family was blessed: kobolds worked hard for their hosts and they would bring good fortune with their magic. But also they were considered the most dangerous and unpredictable of the beings of European folklore. They would taunt and trick and were a great danger to anyone who crossed them.

He wanted to find out how to get rid of them, but there was little that might help. Iron crosses and bells protected you against evil, as did jumping across running water, and self-bored stones and daisy chains, but he couldn't see how any of that would work for him.

It was all . . .

He put his head in his hands, and concentrated on calming his breathing. Cassie would be able to make this stuff sound relevant, but seeing it on these web pages with their picture-book illustrations . . . It seemed so trivial, compared to what had been happening.

He shut down the computer.

None of it seemed real any more. He was overreacting. Getting carried away with it all. He was acting like a baby.

He just needed to sort himself out and it would all be okay.

*

That night, Danny was woken by a strange buzzing sound. He lay in the darkness, his heart racing, his head filled with all kinds of thoughts about what strangeness might be happening now. For a moment, he thought he might be dreaming of Berlin again, the pneumatic drills making holes for more fence posts.

His phone. It was on his bedside cabinet, its vibrations amplified by the wood. He reached for it and squinted at the backlit LCD screen.

He had a text message. He clicked to read it, and saw that the number was blank. How could that be? He OK'd it and the message appeared on screen:

spirit-talking – now

He grunted. It must be Cassie. What did she want?

He turned on the light, found his jeans and a sweatshirt and pulled them on. Stepping into his trainers, he took the office key and went outside.

The crunch of his footsteps in the gravel seemed to reach him from a distance as he crossed the parking area. He wondered, for a moment, if he was dreaming again, but no, it was too real.

He sat in the dark office as the PC started up. He hadn't turned the lights on: he didn't want to draw anyone's attention to his presence in the office.

Start the web browser . . . type the address: www.spirit-talking.co.uk. He was doing this on autopilot, still half asleep.

The site loaded slowly, as before. The stone-effect borders, the smiling photograph of the site's owner, the welcome message –

Danny sat up with a start. The message said: 'Welcome back, Danny.'

Somehow, the site knew who he was, even though he had never told it . . .

He looked at the office door. He was surrounded by darkness, stranded in the pool of light from the computer screen. He couldn't move. He sat with his hand gripping the mouse tightly, knuckles white with the strain.

And as he watched, the mouse pointer crawled across the screen of its own accord. It stopped over the talk boards link. The screen changed and he saw a list of available boards.

He blinked, and found that he could move again.

He should leave. He should just reach down below the desk and press the computer's power button to turn it off.

He looked at the list of talk boards. 'Talk Board #1, Talk Board #2 . . .' And there, at the bottom of the list: 'Danny's Talk Board'. He moved the mouse, clicked, and the chat software started up.

The list on the right told him that the room had two occupants: Lady E and Cynthia. On the main screen a message appeared:

Danny Smith enters at 23:54BST

Cynthia says: Welcome, Danny Smith.

He typed a response, and clicked Send.

Danny Smith says: How do you know my name

Cynthia says: To know others, you must first know yourself.

Lady E says: Who is this? I hear voices. Who are you?

Danny Smith says: Cassie? Is that you? What are you messing about at?

Lady E says: Cassie? Who is this Cassie? Do you mean Konstanz? Konstanz, is that you?

For a moment, Danny had been convinced that Cassie was winding him up – maybe some kind of revenge for their arguing. But Cassie didn't know that Oma's name was Konstanz . . .

Danny Smith says: Eva? Is that you?

Lady E says: Who are you? How do you know my name? What are you doing in my head?

Danny Smith says: It's Danny.

Danny Smith says: I'm your gret nephew. What do you mean in your head?

Cynthia says: Close your eyes and you will see further, Danny Smith.

He stared at the screen, trying to make sense of what was happening. Slowly, the words started to blur so that the letters ran together, merging and separating again so that he felt dizzy. He blinked and rubbed at his eyes.

And when he blinked again his eyes remained shut.

Danny was sitting in a garden, beneath a clear blue sky, apple blossom all around.

Opposite him, sitting with her legs crossed and a checked dress pulled daintily over her knees, was a small blonde girl, aged about seven or eight. She was looking at him expectantly, a faint smile pulling at the corners of her mouth.

There was something familiar about her and suddenly Danny knew that he was looking at his great-aunt. 'Eva? Is that you?'

She nodded, and giggled.

'Your voice,' she said. 'I heard you.' She tapped the side of her head. 'How do you do that?'

'Where is this?' Beyond the apple trees there was a neat kitchen garden, and then a timber house. He heard voices from there, laughter. 'Is this Berlin?'

'I have never been to Berlin,' said Eva.

'But . . . you live there. You *lived* there. When you were older. When I saw you before you were older than this.'

'How could I have been older before? I'll only be older *after*, won't I? That's how it works. Ageing.' She giggled again, an infectious sound, like a musical instrument or an exotic bird call.

Suddenly, she was intense. She leaned forward, her elbows on her knees, her eyes dark and locked on Danny. 'You must trust him, you know. He loves us. He is our protector.'

Danny didn't need to ask who she meant. He was about to protest when little Eva waved a hand and, abruptly, the garden changed.

He was alone now, and the air was heavy with black smoke that burned his throat as he breathed. Sounds of laughter and birdsong had been replaced by the distant wail of sirens and the drone of aircraft high overhead.

A child cried, another murmured softly, and a teenage girl led a younger girl, Eva, round the corner of the house. A teenage boy lay curled up in a ball in the grass, eyes staring and white against his blackened skin, clearly in shock.

Danny looked at the house, now black with smoke, its windows shattered, one wall caved in so that at any moment it might collapse.

'Mama Mama Mama!' little Eva cried, as her sister – Konstanz, Danny realized, his own grandmother – held her and tried to calm her.

Beyond them, another boy limped out of the smoke, emerging from the wreckage of a building. This must be Christian or Dieter. The boy shook his head. 'It is no good,' he said. 'She is dead.'

He must mean their mother – Danny's great-grandmother had died in a bombing raid, he knew. His great-grandfather had died earlier in the war.

'We need help,' Konstanz told her brother. 'It is just us now. We are all that remains of our family.' Four children, orphaned in a war that their country would soon lose, their home in ruins.

At that, Eva stopped crying and looked at the others. 'Hodeken,' she said. 'Will Hodeken help us?'

Konstanz and her older brother exchanged looks. They would humour her. They had to get through this together.

Eva turned to Danny and winked, and it was daylight again, the sky blue, the apple trees in full bloom.

'We called to him,' she said, 'and he came. The others did not believe, at first, but I did. There is much truth hidden in the old stories, and I knew those stories that my mother used to tell me inside out. I knew that if we believed hard enough and our need was great enough then he would come.'

The little girl's intensity was astonishing, her absolute belief in Hodeken. He would answer her call and he would protect them. How could anything resist Eva, even a legendary, powerful creature like Hodeken?

'What did you do?' asked Danny.

'With the last of our supplies we baked him bread, with the last of our water and milk we prepared him a drink, and with the last of our money we laid down an offering. We did this for two nights and he did not come. By the third night, strangely, our belief grew stronger and on this third night of asking he came to us. Without Hodeken we would never have survived the war and the British invasion. We owe him everything. And you do, too. You must trust him, Danny. You have to save the family before it finally tears itself apart. Hodeken always does what is best for us.'

'But what about afterwards? In Berlin, when you all tried to escape and things went wrong. And what about what he did to my father? He drove him mad.'

Eva shrugged. 'I do not know about that. I don't know what happens *after*. Hodeken is our protector. You must trust him, Danny.'

Danny stood, shaking his head. He started to back away.

'Trust him, Danny.'

A hand appeared round the trunk of a craggy old apple tree, and then a cap, a head, a face with crinkly leather skin and bloodshot eyes.

'I told you so,' said the little creature. 'He's blind to the truth. Just like his father was.' He giggled, and then Eva joined in, and the two embraced.

Danny rubbed at his eyes, and when he opened them he was staring at the computer screen.

Lady E leaves at 23:57BST

He slid the pointer across to the exit button and clicked.

Danny Smith leaves at 00:12BST

The screen paused, and then jumped back to the main talk board listings.

He shut the computer down.

As he went across to the door, the memory of Eva's voice came to him again. *You have to save the family before it finally tears itself apart.*

He let himself out into the night.

Trust him, Danny.

16

Keeping It Together

Danny spent Sunday working in the glasshouses, looking after Josh . . . anything that might distract him.

In the evening, he shut himself in his room and tried to do his homework. He had the curtains drawn, and his bedside lamp, the desk lamp and the main light all switched on. The Doors blasted out of the stereo.

And the words on his paper all ran together. Meaningless.

He was tired, and he couldn't concentrate.

She's doing it again.

He put his hands to his temples and pressed, squeezing his head. He had wondered before, so many times, what it must be like to hear the voices his father had heard. The first signs of the madness.

Now he knew.

Home-breaker. Slut. Splitting up the family just like she did last time.

The little voice in his head cut through everything.

What are they doing now?

He pressed harder, but even the blood drumming in his ears was nothing to the nasal tones of his tormentor.

Little Rick had come round earlier, and then he and Val had gone out. For a walk, they said. Just a walk.

Can you picture them, Danny? The two of them? 'Walking'? You know what they're doing, don't you, Danny? You're the one who can stop them. Teach them a lesson.

He grabbed a book and hurled it across the room, pages flapping as it flew through the air.

You don't like it, do you, Danny? She doesn't care about the family.

But it's her life! He wanted to shout it out loud, but he knew that would not stop the voice in his head.

Let her choose. It was none of his business.

He stood, knocking his chair over.

Out, down the stairs, into the night.

Fresh air – he had thought that maybe the air would clear his head, but it was a muggy night, the air heavy and warm. Somewhere in the village a car tooted its horn three times.

Silence.

He breathed deeply. He rubbed at his face. He had been crying.

He was cracking up.

Just like his father had.

Still, there was silence.

Then he heard voices. Raised – arguing? Excited?

He walked round to the side of the Hall, to where the lawns rolled down towards the lake.

There were two figures down there, beyond the marquee. They could only be Val and Rick.

He wanted to turn away. Leave them to it. Their lives.

But instead, he stepped towards the tall privet hedge that ran down one side of the grass. The ground was clear behind it, where nothing would grow in its shade. It made a rough path.

He walked along, behind the hedge, to a gap halfway down.

Straight across from where he stood, the marquee loomed large and almost luminously white in the darkness.

Val and Rick were by the water.

They were still arguing, but more quietly now. Their voices were urgent, harsh, but Danny could not make out their words.

He watched as Rick seized Val's arms and she pushed him away, then he seized her again and she relaxed. Their voices were briefly silenced, before Rick started again, more softly.

Slut.

Danny wanted to turn away, but he could not.

He watched as Rick held his mother. Val stood stiffly, looking over Rick's shoulder.

He couldn't work out what was going on. There were tensions and hidden meanings he could not make sense of.

Home-breaker.

The gap in the hedge was where a path led through to the main area of vegetable plots.

Someone had been dumping rocks here, debris from digging. Danny squatted.

Some of the rocks were fist-sized, rough-edged.

Go on. Scare them, Danny. Teach them a lesson!

The only sound now was the pounding in his head.

Stop them, Danny.

He picked up one of the stones.

Put a stop to this.

He stared at the rock, at the way its rough surface picked up the moonlight.

He breathed deeply, steadily.

'What's this? What are you doing?'

He looked up. It was Luke, peering at him in the gloom.

Slowly, Danny opened his hand, tipped it, and the stone tumbled to the ground.

Luke taught the lunar-gardening courses for the Hope Springs Trust: growing crops by the cycles of the moon.

'What are you sneaking around here for?' Luke had a penlight, and he flicked it on, shining it towards Danny.

Danny raised a hand, shielding his eyes from the light.

He stood, backed away, then turned and ran as fast as he could, as if by running he might leave everything behind.

Early the next morning he heard voices raised outside.

He had slept fitfully, twisting and turning through the night, waking in a tangle of duvet and sheet.

The voice in his head remained silent, but all the time he knew that somewhere nearby – in the flat, he was sure – Hodeken was lurking. Hiding. Waiting for his next opportunity to taunt Danny.

Each time he had woken, he had done so with a vivid fragment of dream in his head. The moonlight, the privet hedge, a rock nestled in the cup of his hand. He could remember that rock's rough surface, its weight as he held it.

He had been close to losing it last night. The self-control he had built up to protect himself was nothing to the siren call of Hodeken's voice in his head.

He had been unable to resist.

What might have happened, if Luke had not come along and seen him?

What might he have done?

Sharmila called up the stairs to Val.

'What's up?' Danny said, peering round his half-open door at Val, who stood on the landing, leaning down over the stair rail to listen to Sharmila.

'The marquee,' she said, turning. 'Problems. I don't know what, exactly.' She looked rough, her face pale and big shadows under her eyes.

Danny pulled on some clothes, and followed Val and Josh down the stairs. He walked across the car park, still puzzled, wondering what might have happened.

He looked round the corner of the Hall and . . . the marquee had vanished.

No – it was just that it was no longer visible above the rose and honeysuckle hedge. As he approached the lawn, he saw that the marquee had, in fact, collapsed.

David was there, a gaunt man with silver hair and a pointed beard. He stood with his hands on his hips as Sharmila joined him and put her arms round his waist. Rick and Warren were down on the far side of the fallen marquee, pulling at the white canvas as if trying to see inside. Tim and Won't were there, too, pushing each other and watching Jade, who had come down here in just shorts and a T-shirt, hair wet from the shower.

'What happened?' asked Val.

'Kids from the village,' said David. 'Some kind of prank, I'd say. I don't think there's any actual damage. I've called the people who supplied the marquee, and left a message on their answerphone asking them to come out and help us get it back up. I think we need a community gathering, too. It's just kids, I'm sure, but this may be a symptom of bad feeling in the wider community. We should work through the issues together.'

'When you left your message,' said Rick, coming up to join them, 'did you ask them to bring any tent pegs? Someone's nicked them all.'

Danny just stood and stared at the fallen marquee. It humped up in the middle, where some of the poles had fallen over the trestle tables that had been inside.

It had been fine last night.

David had described it as some kind of prank. Danny's mind raced. Hodeken was a joker, a prankster.

Could this be his work?

Back in the flat, Danny rushed to get ready for school. He was late.

He pulled on his shirt and looped the ready-knotted tie over his head. He took his blazer from the wardrobe, although it would be too warm today to wear it before he reached the school gates and had to put it on.

His bag. He reached up to the cupboard over the

wardrobe, pulled the door open, and a shower of heavy metal tent pegs tipped out on to him.

He put an arm up to protect himself, and staggered back.

An instant later, he stepped over the pegs and shut the bedroom door so no one would see.

There were hundreds of the things, some still with moist earth stuck to them.

Hodeken!

He reached up, took his bag, and put his books in it for today.

What to do with the pegs?

There was nothing to put them in, so he took his sleeping bag and started to put them in there. When it was full, he put it into the wardrobe and managed to shut the doors.

17

Gather and Share

It was late, and he walked to school on his own. Rick had driven the Mini, and Tim, Won't and Jade had all piled in. They could have fitted Danny in, at a squeeze, but when he saw them in the car park he'd slipped away through the trees, avoiding them.

He walked with his blazer slung over his shoulder and his bag dangling.

There was a great pressure in his head, a sense that things were building up.

Soon, something must give.

He turned on to the track across the fields, and as he walked he listened.

There was a faint whistling of tinnitus in his ear but nothing else from within. The only sounds were the wind in the branches of the trees that lined the brook, the ceaseless droning of a wood pigeon, the occasional bursts of song from greenfinches and blackcaps, the traffic on the main road. All the normal sounds of the countryside in late spring.

No voice.

Was Hodeken resting, or simply biding his time?

Danny reached Morses Lane, hesitated, and then turned right.

He couldn't face school today. He couldn't think straight. He couldn't imagine sitting in a class thinking about trigonometry or Shakespeare and all the time, just waiting . . . waiting for the voice to start up.

The road cut through an industrial estate. In the lane by the tyre-fitter's, he paused and stuffed his blazer and tie into his bag. He knew he would still look like a fourteen-year-old bunking off school, but it was a little less obvious now.

When he came to the New Meade Estate, he was sure everyone was looking at him. The old man mowing his tiny front lawn. The young mum holding a baby in the window of one of the small, modern houses. The teenager in blue overalls who passed him heading the other way and didn't look much older than Danny. The postwoman wheeling her bicycle along the pavement from house to house.

All staring.

He studied the cracks in the pavement as he walked, head down, trying to blend in.

He had never done this before.

He felt terribly exposed.

Across the estate, there was a track down past the allotments to the river. Away from the houses, he felt less vulnerable, but still this felt wrong.

It was a mistake. He knew that now. Ahead of him,

he had a day on his own, just himself and the thoughts in his head.

'So. Where have you been, then?'

Val stared at him, her arms crossed.

Danny slung his bag through the open door of his bedroom.

'What?'

'Don't you "what" me. Why weren't you at school today?'

He walked past her, into his room. He took his blazer off and made as if to put it in the wardrobe, then stopped himself, remembering the sleeping bag full of the marquee's pegs. He dumped it across his chair instead.

He turned, and she was in the doorway, leaning against the frame.

'So?' she said.

He turned away from her again, and went to sit in the window seat.

'Rick came round. He thought you were sick. I didn't know what he was talking about.'

He felt a sudden twinge of something, deep inside his head. A stirring. He breathed deeply, and held the air in his lungs. Then out again, and held.

'So?' she said again.

He looked at her. He remembered the stone, heavy in his hand last night. He blinked. 'I'm sorry,' he said, finally. 'I won't do it again.'

Later, he went out to the kitchen to make himself a sandwich. Val was there, putting a load into the washing machine. She looked up at him. 'You going to the Gather and Share tonight?' she said brightly. 'It's at six thirty.'

He shrugged. He wasn't sure if he could face a gathering of the residents of Hope Springs.

'Hey, did you see they'd put the marquee back up today?' she added. 'We found the pegs this morning.'

He stared at her.

She was smiling, trying to be positive. There was no hint of accusation in her expression.

'I . . .' He stopped. He didn't know what he had been going to say.

'They were in the woods,' Val went on. 'All of them, hammered into the ground in circles, like fairy rings.'

He made his sandwich, then went back to his room with it. With the door closed, he went to the wardrobe. He opened it carefully, remembering the cascade of pegs when he had opened the cupboard above it this morning.

His sleeping bag was there, but it was empty, slumped on top of a stack of shoes. He picked it up. There was mud inside it, but no pegs.

Hodeken, up to his tricks again.

They sat on plastic chairs arranged in a circle in the old school refectory. That was the Hope Springs way: in a circle everyone was equal.

Despite this, they all turned to David to start the meeting. They might have no leader, but David was the one who had founded Hope Springs, and the Hope Springs Trust had been created round his ideals and ideas.

Danny took one of the few remaining seats. There was

a good turnout tonight. Most of the adults were there. Jade, Won't and Tim were there, too, and Josh sat on the floor at Val's feet, grinning evilly and trying to twist the head off a rag doll.

'Okay, okay,' said David, holding his hands up, palms outward, to get people's attention. He spoke softly, but his voice carried clearly round the group, easily expanding to fill the tall-ceilinged room.

'Is it okay with everybody if we begin? We have some issues to get through here tonight. If it's okay with everybody, I'd like to raise the practical details of Saturday's open day stroke village fête, but first of all I'd like to initiate a discussion of HoST's relations with the wider community, using the marquee incident as a sounding point. But also, in accordance with our constitution, as this is a formal gathering of the Trust's residents, this is the opportunity to explore any other issues you may have brought with you, and to share thoughts, feelings and experiences with us all. Okay, then? Shall we begin?'

Danny sat and listened and watched. Val had taken a seat a short distance from Rick rather than taking the empty seat next to him, where Sunil now sat. There was a lot about Rick and Val that Danny didn't understand, a tension that seemed to run between them whenever they were together.

It must be lurrrrve.

He put a hand to his forehead. The voice ... it was back.

'... the owners of the marquee have very kindly waived any charge for coming and sorting it out today,'

David was saying. 'Which saves us having to confront the issue of whose responsibility such a charge would have been. The Village Fête Committee hired the marquee, but it's on land we look after, so it's not clear where responsibilities lie.'

'We should post guards,' said Sunil, leaning forward in his chair, staring round the gathering through his tiny circular spectacles. 'Fend the buggers off, I say.'

Sharmila swept beaded hair back from her slender, lined face and smiled warmly at Sunil. 'With respect,' she said, 'that is hardly the most enlightened approach. The question this raises in my mind is how this incident reflects on our relationship with the village. We're holding this open event to stimulate local interest in the alternatives we offer, but was this just a practical joke or was it some kind of gesture?'

'Why not ask Daniel Smith?'

Everyone turned towards Luke, who had just spoken. He fiddled with his moustache, and nodded towards Danny. 'He was out there last night, sneaking around. Hiding in the bushes by the path into the lunar-gardening plots.'

'Is that right, Danny?' asked David, fixing him with his pale blue eyes. 'When was this?'

'A-about half ten,' said Danny. 'I went out for a walk.' It sounded lame. He knew they were accusing him, blaming him.

'And what happened?'

'Nothing. I saw Luke. The marquee was still up. Nothing.'

'He ran away when I caught him,' said Luke. 'He did a runner, didn't he?'

Danny didn't know where to look. They were all staring. Accusing him.

See where it gets you if you don't trust old Hodeken?

His skin was burning, and he knew that made him look guilty, but knowing that only made it so much worse.

Why was this silence dragging out? Why would nobody say anything?

You don't like it when I talk to you. You don't listen to me. You don't trust me and, like I told you, if you don't trust me things might go wrong. Like your grandfather, shot in the river. Like your father . . .

Little Rick was speaking. Danny tried to block out the taunting voice in his head.

'. . . were out around then,' Rick said. 'Weren't we, Val, love?'

Danny's mother was staring at the wood tiles of the refectory floor.

'You must have seen us, Danny,' Rick continued. 'You must almost have bumped into us.'

Rick was staring at Danny now, another accusing look. But he was accusing Danny of something different.

He knows, Hodeken chanted. *He knows you were following them. He's scared of you now, Danny. We'll see him off yet!*

Danny couldn't look away from him, but he couldn't answer, either. He felt well and truly trapped.

Then, at last, Little Rick smiled, breaking the spell.

'So if anything had happened while Danny was

there we'd have all seen it, wouldn't we? It must have happened later.'

'He could have sneaked back afterwards,' said Luke, unwilling to give up.

Little Rick raised his hands, just as his father had raised his hands for attention earlier. 'Go easy on him, Lucas,' he said. 'Danny's had a hard time. He's been through a lot. They *all* have, haven't you, Val?'

Danny looked at his mother. She was staring at Rick, willing him to say no more.

He knows everything, the voice told Danny.

'I think we're moving away from the purpose of this discussion,' said Sharmila. 'I'm not sure now is the time to discuss the wider implications of the incident with the marquee, after all. We would only be speculating. Let's focus on the positive, the coming together of Hope Springs and Wishbourne on Saturday.' She sat back and smiled encouragingly into the silence that followed her intervention.

'I still think we should post guards,' said Sunil, and then Warren asked for volunteers to help him organize the stall that would give away HoST produce to their neighbours and, slowly, the meeting moved on.

Danny sat through it all, saying little, still convinced that whenever anyone looked in his direction it was an accusing look, a challenge.

At the end, as everyone started to leave, Sharmila caught Danny's eye. 'Hey,' she said, bringing her hands together in front of her chest. 'Danny. Give me a hand with the chairs?'

He nodded, and picked up the nearest chair and stacked it on the next one along.

'You didn't share much tonight,' said Sharmila. 'You hold everything within, don't you? You think that's a good thing?'

It was how he coped. He said nothing, which was probably answer enough.

'I didn't know Rick and your mother were an item, if that is still the phrase.'

'Are they?' He dragged a stack of chairs across the floor, then paused to pick them up when they made too loud a scraping noise.

'You don't know? Aren't you interested? You're not much of a gossip! I thought you would spill all the beans for me.'

She was trying to be jolly but there was something not quite right. Danny couldn't work out what it was.

'They're both single,' he said. 'They can do what they like.' And all the time, trying desperately to block the little voice in his head.

'As long as you're okay with it. You seem troubled, though.'

'I'm a teenager,' said Danny. 'It goes with the territory.'

Sharmila laughed. Then she said, 'Danny, if there are any problems, you would tell me, wouldn't you?'

'What sort of problems?'

'Well . . . it's just . . . You know I am not David's first partner?'

Danny nodded, thrown a little by the sudden change of direction.

'David is an intense man. Very focused. It is one of his strengths. Only . . . when I first knew him this was more extreme. He was an obsessive man. One reason the school closed was that he was such a perfectionist he drove his best staff away with his demands and his expectations. He drove Ruby away, too – Rick's mother. He always found fault in what others did, he fussed over every detail, he was convinced that where the world did not meet his high standards he could make it do so simply by applying his own will. Everything collapsed around him. He lost his wife and his school and he has had to reconstruct both himself and his life from all that went wrong. He is an entirely different man now.'

She stopped, and Danny watched her, his eyebrows raised. 'And?' he prompted her.

'Rick . . . he has had problems,' said Sharmila. 'He is like his father was, only perhaps more so. I'm sure he's fine with your mother and I wish them well. But Rick can be very single-minded at times. Like I say, I'm sure everything will be fine. I shouldn't be saying all this, but hey, I gossip.'

She smiled. 'You will tell me, won't you, if there's anything I should know?'

Danny nodded.

'Good. I will talk to David. He is a calming influence on Rick. He will tell me I am being silly.'

18

A Little Word in Your Ear, Danny

'Is it catching?'

Cassie. Round the back of the science block, throwing him with her questions again.

She laughed. 'Whatever it was you had on Monday.'

He'd come round here to get away from Won't and Jase and the others. He just wanted a peaceful lunch break. He hadn't been ready for this.

He kicked at the ground.

'You were on the hop, weren't you? Skipping off. You'll be in deep do if they catch you. I thought you were smarter than that, Danny Schmidt.'

He looked up now, at her use of his name. She was smirking.

She's not a looker now, is she?

The voice in his head . . . spying. Taunting him. Hodeken had been quiet until now.

'You're no more talkative, are you? You can take the strong silent act too far, you know.'

He shrugged and looked away, across the playing fields to where the trees marked the bank of the river.

'How have things been?' Cassie asked, after a long

silence. 'You know . . . After the chat room. You can tell me now, you know.'

'Tell you what?'

'That it was a set-up. That you typed all those messages and you made it all up just to wind me up. I tell you, German Danny, you really had me going for a while there. You really fooled me.'

He shook his head, and walked away from her.

He couldn't take this right now.

He didn't understand her. He never knew when she was serious or when she was joking. She did things to his head.

Women. They're half the problem, eh?

He shook his head, as if that might rattle something loose.

Later, sitting at the foot of a tree, his phone vibrated in his pocket. Cassie.

Call me if u wnt. C

He saved the message, then turned the phone off and put it away. He breathed deeply and held the breath in so that he felt his lungs pushing harder, harder against his ribs and the base of his throat. He breathed out and held.

His head was calm. His head was empty of thoughts. He was in control.

See? You can do it when you want.

At the end of the day, Danny's maths teacher, Ms Nesbitt, caught him just as he was leaving the classroom. 'Danny,' she said, holding a hand up, a finger pointing towards the ceiling.

He stopped, waited.

'Mr Sullivan asked me to pass on a message to you. Would you call in and see him before you leave? He'll be in S106, or the prep room next door.'

Danny nodded and left the room. Little Rick probably had the Mini again, and was going to offer him a lift. He was tempted not to go and see him. He would walk home instead. But he'd be in trouble if Rick waited around for him and he never showed up.

He headed downstairs, part of the general rush for the exits. Then he turned back against the flow, and headed through to the science block.

At first he thought the lab was empty. The stools were neatly arranged, tucked under the benches, everything tidied away into plastic drawers and glass cabinets. Even the locust tank looked neat and ordered.

Rick was over in the far corner. He raised a lazy hand just as Danny spotted him. He had a cup of coffee, but he hadn't drunk any.

'Danny,' he said. 'I'm glad you could come. Here, take a seat.' He pushed a stool out with one foot, and it tipped, wobbled as if it were going to fall over, then righted itself.

Danny dropped his bag on the floor and sat. Through the blinds he could see the crowds of children pushing and jostling in the queues for the buses.

'Good day?' asked Rick, adjusting his ponytail so that it lay straight between his shoulder blades.

'Okay,' said Danny. 'You know how it is.'

'Yeah.' Rick laughed. 'I do, Danny, I do.'

A murmur of voices rose in the corridor, then passed, fading away to nothing.

'You're doing okay here, aren't you, Danny?'

This was about him bunking off on Monday, Danny realized. A friendly chat. Make sure there aren't any major problems, make sure he doesn't do it again.

'You do well in most subjects, don't you? You do enough without ever giving a hundred per cent. You don't want to stand out, although you probably could. You keep your head down. Some good friends, too. How long have you been here at Severnside? About six months?'

Danny nodded. Outside, two of the buses had arrived and the crowd had thinned. The sky was a heavy grey in the direction of Wishbourne. It looked as if it might be a wet walk home if he didn't get out of here soon.

'You were following us, weren't you?'

Danny looked up. Rick was staring at him, eyes narrowed, a half-smile fixed on his face.

'I . . .'

'Now why would you be doing something like that? It's not healthy, is it, Danny? It's not good.'

Rick picked up his cup of coffee, blew on it and sipped, blew on it and sipped again.

'You're a bright lad, aren't you, Danny? We've already covered that ground. We know you're bright, when you want to be. That's good. It means I can explain a few truths to you, Danny, and you're bright enough to understand what I'm saying. Is that okay? Danny? Is that okay?'

Danny nodded, once. He tried to swallow, but his throat was dry, clogged up.

'Good.' Rick raised his cup, blew on the coffee and sipped. Carefully, he lowered the cup and placed it on the bench, in the exact position it had occupied before. 'I've had a difficult life, Danny. It's okay: I don't expect sympathy. I'm just setting this in context for you, so you can see where I'm coming from.'

He raised his cup, blew, sipped, and then put it back in its place on the workbench.

'David,' Rick chuckled. 'He made life hell for me. And for Mum. He drove her away, and he'd have driven me away too if I could have gone. Instead, I stayed and grew up with his put-downs and his stupid rules and whims. I've never been very successful with the ladies, you know? Would you believe that? I've tried. Oh, I've tried everything, but it's never lasted. I always blamed myself. But now, Danny, do you know what has happened? Do you?'

He waited until Danny shook his head.

'I came to a new understanding, a realization. I saw that the problem had simply been that I had never found the right woman. And do you know what it was that made me realize that? Val. Your mother, Danny.'

Outside, the last of the buses arrived. Children filed on to it and the bus pulled away.

'You don't want to hear all this, do you, Danny? You don't want to think about these things – people my age, your mother . . . But, Danny, you have to. I have to make you understand how things are. You see, Sharmila spoke to me about all this last night. She asked how things were, and she let slip that you're bothered by my relationship with your mother.

'That's only natural, Danny. You're protective. You've been through a lot in the last few years and you don't want to let anyone in. But Danny, I hope you'll be on my side. I hope we can still be friends.

'Because ... I'm not going to let anything stand in my way. Do you understand? The course of love can be difficult at times, but I am determined. I won't give in. If you have a problem with that then you need to sort yourself out.'

He raised his cup, blew, sipped.

'I know what happened, Danny. I know your dad's inside. I know what you went through at your old school. You don't want that to start again here, do you? All the attention, all the exposure. And just think what it'd do to Val ... I can help you, Danny. I'm good at helping people – that's why I'm a teacher. Do you want me to help you, Danny, or do you want me as an enemy? I won't allow you to stand in my way. I'm a teacher, Danny. I could make life very difficult for you here, if I had to. If I were forced to. I don't want to do that. I'd much rather help you.'

Danny sat on the stool in the science lab, and stared at him. Rick. Mr Sullivan.

There was a madness in his eyes.

Danny knew about these things.

Just then, a little voice somewhere deep in his head said softly, *I told you so. You should have believed me. You should have trusted me. You should have scared him off when you had the chance.*

'We're late,' said Rick, pausing to finish his coffee. He smiled, and straightened his ponytail. 'I've got the Mini. Do you want a lift? No? You're walking in this?' He gestured at the window with an open hand. It was raining hard outside, all of a sudden. Fierce golden sunlight lit the school buildings against the heavy grey ceiling of the sky.

Danny gathered his bag and threaded his way through the benches to the door. As he left the room he glanced back and Rick was watching him, smiling like an old friend.

Outside, great gobs of rain assaulted him, plastering his hair to his skull, stunning his senses with its ferocity.

He walked, barely noticing.

'Look at you!' said Val from the top of the stairs, when she saw him enter the flat.

Danny looked up at her, then down at himself. He was soaked through.

'You get those things straight off, do you hear? You'll have *ruined* that blazer! You drop everything where you are and I'll get a hot shower going for you.'

He dropped his bag. He tried to shrug himself out of the blazer, but it was too tight and it was sticking to him with the rain. He hauled it off and let it fall on the doormat.

'Go on. The lot.'

He turned his back, then stooped to unravel his

shoelaces. There was a pool of water round him on the tiled floor.

Once out of his trousers and his shirt, there was a sudden, soft thud in his back. He twisted and caught the bath towel before it could fall to the ground.

He peered up the stairs through his wet fringe. Val was smiling. 'Okay, that's enough,' she said. 'The shower's running. You're allowed up.'

All of a sudden, he wanted to tell her. Right here. Shout it up the stairs if needs be.

About the voices in his head, about the struggle he was having to keep tight control. He wanted to tell her about Rick. Tell her what he was really like.

She was still smiling, waiting.

He couldn't.

It was her life.

He dipped his head, and climbed the stairs.

Late in the afternoon, dry and dressed from the shower, Danny answered the phone. He was half expecting it to be his father. It had been a while since he had called.

'Hello, is that Daniel Smith?'

'Yes. Yes it is.'

'Ah, good. It's Justin Peters here. I don't know if you remember me . . . the barrister. How are you?'

'Okay,' said Danny. 'Not bad.'

'Is your mother there?'

Danny went through to the kitchen, where Val was sipping at a mug of herbal tea. He handed the phone to her, and sat down at the table.

'Mm-hm,' she said. 'Yes, that's right.'

The appeal, Danny thought. This must be about the appeal. He tried to read his mother's expression, but couldn't.

'I see. So that's it?' A long pause, as Mr Peters explained something. 'Okay. Thank you. Thanks for letting us know.'

She pressed the disconnect button on the handset and placed the phone on the table.

'That was your father's barrister,' she said.

'I know. What's happening?'

'He says the appeal isn't going to be pursued.'

'*No!*'

Danny twisted in his seat. Oma Schmidt was standing in the doorway, her mouth open. 'No,' she said again, more softly this time. She looked very small and old, just then.

Danny stood and went to her, held her. She felt rigid in his arms, trembling like a trapped animal.

'Why?' he said, looking back at Val. 'What changed their minds?'

'Mr Peters said the new evidence was too flimsy to construct a good case. The journal. It doesn't add enough that's new to demonstrate a miscarriage of justice, he said. And he said that your father's been behaving erratically. Was he okay last time you visited? You didn't say anything.'

'You didn't ask.'

'No,' she said, shaking her head and looking down. 'I didn't, did I?'

'No,' moaned Oma again, sobbing now, her tears soaking through Danny's dry shirt. '*Mein Junge.* I want my boy. I do not want to see him in that place. I want my boy!'

Danny exchanged a look with his mother.

Oma had been clinging to the idea of this appeal. They were never likely to release Danny's father, but for a time it had given Oma some kind of hope.

It was her age, Danny realized. That was why this was so critical to her. She would die with her family divided and her son locked away in prison. Nothing would change that.

'We'll see him again soon,' said Danny, into his grandmother's white hair. 'You can find one of your old pictures and we'll take it and you can talk about the old times. He'll like that. You always make him happy.'

'You think?'

Just then there was a thud from below, as the front door opened and shut.

'Hello, everyone,' Little Rick called up the stairs. 'Only me.'

He came up, and stopped on the landing, with Danny and Oma standing in the kitchen doorway.

'Hey, Danny,' he said, smiling. 'You must have got a good soaking tonight. Did you?' He patted Danny on the arm, just like old friends. Mates. 'You should have taken up my offer of a lift. Isn't that right, Val? He should have come back with me in the car.'

He grinned. In the kitchen Val was still sitting quietly, staring down at the phone.

'What's up, Val?' said Rick, brushing past Danny into the kitchen. 'Did your ex break out of the nick, or something?'

At that, Oma pushed away from Danny and headed in the direction of her room. Danny watched her retreat, then he looked into the kitchen.

With a quick flick of his head and a movement of his eyes, Rick indicated that Danny should go. This was his territory now and he didn't want Danny in the way.

19
Open Day

He slept and, once again, he dreamed of Hodeken.

Danny sat at the foot of a huge, towering tree, so big that its roots spread out around him like a cathedral's buttresses, each as broad as a normal tree's trunk.

In front of him there was a big wooden tent peg stuck in the leaf litter. Somewhere, a woodpecker drummed on a dead tree, the sound reminding him of pneumatic drills in the streets and another dream altogether.

He stood and pulled the peg from the ground. A short distance away he saw another. He went over to it and pulled it out. He put both pegs into his coat pocket. It seemed important to be tidy.

He looked around, and there was another. He pulled it, and continued on his way, gathering the pegs and taking them with him as he went.

He came to a stream, and decided to follow it up the hill. There must be a spring somewhere. He seemed to remember looking for a spring one time before.

Through the trees! A tune. A familiar tune: one of the old German folk tunes that Oma sang. He felt the magic in the music now, the calming influence. He pulled himself up the slope past a young tree, and paused. There was a wall of rock before him, a little cliff set into the hillside, and from its base the stream burst out.

So this was the beginning of things, the spring.

For a moment, he thought what he had taken to be music was actually the merry gurgling of the spring, but then he saw that there was a dark crack in the cliff, and perched on a boulder by that cavern there was a small figure, its head partly hidden by a conical, grey felt hat. The music was coming from this figure – Hodeken's head bobbed from side to side as he hummed.

Danny took the pegs from his pocket and laid them carefully at the base of this boulder, his work complete.

'Very good,' said that nasal voice. 'I'd grant you a wish. But then I was granting you a wish anyway. I haven't forgotten.' Hodeken sprang down from the rock and stood so that Danny now had to peer down at him.

'Forgotten?' asked Danny.

'Your wish,' said Hodeken. 'Remember? You want everything to be how it was.'

'But it can't,' said Danny. 'That's not possible.'

'Don't give up so easily,' said Hodeken, skipping back up on to his rock again, so that now he looked down at Danny. 'Okay, I'll confess: things are more complicated in this modern world of yours. It takes some working out. But we can do it, Danny. We can fix everything. I just need your help.'

Help?

'The first thing to do is to get rid of Rick.'

Danny shook his head. Hodeken's words sounded

ominously final. Was this what he had done to Danny's father? Whispering suggestions, instructions, haunting his sleep until he cracked. 'It's her choice,' he said. 'It's nothing to do with me.'

'Oh very admirable, Danny. Well done! But we both know that he's wrong for her, don't we? And how will your wish ever come true while he's around? Trust me, Danny. I'm doing what's best for you all. Sometimes you have to act in other people's interests when you know what's best.'

With that, the little man jumped down so that he clung to Danny's collar with his feet on Danny's hips and stared him in the eye.

'Look at me, Danny. I'm ancient! You're a child, Danny. You all are to someone like me. Trust me, boy. I know what's best. Do what I say and we'll fix it together.'

He hopped off Danny, down to the ground.

'Look,' he said, pointing to where Danny had laid the pegs. 'You missed one.'

Danny turned and saw a peg still in the ground. He stooped to collect it and there was a sudden weight at his back, pushing him. He sprawled in the dirt, gasping for air.

When he looked up, Hodeken had vanished and he was alone in the woods.

He gathered himself up. He didn't want to be here.

Trust me.

No. He started to walk through the trees, and then to run, desperate to get away from here.

Do as I say, Danny. It'll be okay.

No. No! Nooooo!

He woke.

Again and again, he woke, and each time his head was filled with the dying echoes of Hodeken's thin voice.

His father had been an ordinary man. He often didn't notice what was going on around him, and he forgot birthdays and anniversaries. He was prone to the occasional outburst of temper, but he seemed reasonably happy in his job and in his family life. But then he had changed.

Val had started to neglect him, and Eva and Oma had taken to pointing this out to him and slowly, ever so slowly, his life had started to fall apart around him.

He had cracked.

The voices in his head had done it, pushed him over the edge.

Danny lay there, in the dark hours of the night, and he wondered how much of this he could take before he, too, gave way.

If it had broken his father, then what chance did Danny have?

Finally, he woke and there was silence in his head.

He climbed out of bed and went to the window. Dawn had already broken outside, the morning light bright through the trees.

He pulled on his clothes and trainers and went outside.

The air was fresh, as if it had rained overnight. It was Saturday morning, he remembered. The day of the open day.

Suddenly, he remembered the dream, gathering all those wooden tent pegs. He rushed across the car park and peered over the rose and honeysuckle hedge.

The marquee was still standing.

The grass shimmered with moisture – either rain or dew, he wasn't sure which.

He breathed deep, and savoured the stillness of the early morning. Maybe things would work out. Maybe this was some kind of turning point.

He went back inside.

The weather was cool but sunny and promising to turn into a real scorcher. Everyone was sure the Bank Holiday Saturday crowds would be tempted out of their homes for the open day.

One of the local farmers had set aside a field at the back of Wishbourne Hall for parking, and Danny helped Won't and Sunil guide the cars in, and hand out leaflets listing the day's attractions and a map of the grounds. They were collecting money, too. HoST had agreed with the Fête Committee that entry would be free, but they would charge for parking, encouraging people to use alternative means of transport.

Won't was grumbling about their work almost from the start. 'How come we get this, then?' he said.

'Smile,' Sunil told him. 'We form the first impression of Hope Springs for our guests. Be happy!'

Danny quite enjoyed the routine of it. Filling up the field from the front. Making sure there were sensible routes through the parked cars and no one was blocked in. He liked the buzz of anticipation of people arriving for a day out.

He liked the silence in his head.

By mid-morning the field was half full and Martin and Tim had come to take over car-park duties.

Danny wandered back with Won't through the wooded area towards the marquee. There were people everywhere. Lots of them were following the garden trail indicated on the leaflet's map of the grounds, but others were just wandering, having a good look.

'So, is Cassie going to be here, then?' asked Won't.

Danny shrugged. 'I don't know,' he said.

'Thought you might. Thought you might be meeting her. You two being –'

'Being what?'

Won't sniggered, but said no more.

They came to the hedge at the top of the lawns, and Danny surveyed the crowd. Lots of old people. Families with children rushing about. Residents of Hope Springs and the rest of the village standing behind stalls with plants for sale, a tombola, a raffle, a bouncy castle and bric-a-brac stalls.

The jangling sound of sitar music drifted across from the marquee. David must have put one of his CDs on.

No sign of Cassie. He didn't know if she would be here today or not. He hadn't seen her to ask.

'Come on, they'll be wondering where we've got to,' said Danny, heading down the slope towards the marquee.

*

The marquee was lined with trestle tables displaying the flowers and vegetables entered in the village show. Giant cabbages and leeks sat side by side with fussy arrangements of late spring flowers and handicrafts. Off on another set of tables Warren was giving away bags full of Hope Springs produce – all organic – accompanied by a leaflet outlining the courses and activities on offer at HoST. There was a children's art show at one end of the tent, and at the other were tables and chairs where HoST were providing refreshments.

'How did we do it?' complained Won't. 'We get the car parking just when people are arriving, and now we're working on refreshments just as lunchtime's coming up . . . Someone has it in for us.'

Danny got stuck in behind the scenes, ladling carrot and coriander soup into bowls, emptying the used grounds from the coffee machine and refilling it.

Again, he lost himself in the routine activity. He even found himself humming a little tune as he worked.

He stopped, panicking, when he recognized the tune. One of Oma's – one she must have learned from Hodeken.

Nothing.

Just the buzz of voices, the pleasant wash of sitars and tabla . . . in his head: silence.

Later, he saw Cassie standing in the queue with her parents.

She may have spotted him. He didn't know. He concentrated on what he was doing.

'Hey, Danny. Would you fetch some more rolls from

the kitchen?' called Warren, across the food preparation area, late in the afternoon. 'We're running out. Jade's up there. She'll sort them out for you.'

He went, glad to escape the heat of the gas stove.

Outside, the sun burned down, harsh and bright.

He cut across the main lawn, through the stalls and the crowds. Lots of people had settled down on the grass to picnic. David was strolling through, juggling and balloon-modelling for the children.

It reminded Danny of childhood visits to the south coast at the height of summer. Ice creams and slot machines and those heaving, hot crowds. Those trips had always been fun.

Round the back of the Hall, he mounted the steps to the kitchen.

Jade was there, dusting icing sugar over another tray of cakes for the refreshments. She hadn't noticed him come in.

Danny looked around at the chaos of the kitchen. Pots and pans everywhere. Three black bin liners full of rubbish. People had been working here since the crack of dawn, he knew.

'Hi,' said Danny.

Jade started, and looked round.

'Gave me a fright,' she said, flicking a strand of hair away from her eyes.

Danny let his eyes roam around the kitchen again. 'I was looking for more bread rolls,' he said. 'But . . .'

She grinned, pointed. 'There, by the pastries. Under the cloth.'

Danny went over and lifted the corner of a sheet of muslin. There was a tray stacked with rolls: white, wholemeal, some flecked with herbs.

'What d'you reckon? I made them last night.'

'They look good.'

He tucked the cloth back over them, and slid the tray out to make it easier to pick up.

'Couldn't get the door, could you?'

She went over, reached out for the handle, and then paused. 'You need to get rid of him, you know,' she said, in a friendly, reasonable tone.

Danny stopped and looked at her.

Her wide, dark eyes stared at him intently. Her lips were slightly parted, as if she was about to add something.

'Rick,' she said, finally. 'You need to get him out of the way.'

'I . . .'

He wanted to barge past her, run like hell, but he had the tray, the rolls. He had a job to do. He couldn't just . . .

'Do it, Danny. It's gone too far now. You have to get rid of him.'

He was pressing up against a work surface, as far from her as he could be without actually backing off into the kitchen.

Her eyes . . .

Jade's eyes had gone pale, the irises tiny black dots. The whites of her eyes, so pure before, were now a tapestry of fine red blood vessels.

As he watched, the smooth skin of her face became

tough, leathery, landscaped with lines and lumps and tiny hairy growths.

And her mouth! Now it was a narrow slit, the lips almost vanished, the teeth small, yellow, crooked.

Suddenly he was aware that there was a kitchen knife on the work surface behind him. Black-handled, with a long, wedge-shaped blade. He wanted to reach for it. Protection.

He felt dizzy. He felt a madness rising.

He was clutching the tray so tightly its edges felt in danger of breaking his skin.

He needed to stop this. Stop it now.

He struggled to breathe, and looked again at the grotesque creature before him.

'Trust me,' it said, and Jade's voice had become higher-pitched, nasal, more penetrating.

And then she leaned towards the door, pulled at it, stepped back, and she was Jade again, and outside sunlight flooded the yard behind the Hall and birds sang from high in the trees.

He stumbled past her, out into the fresh air.

He crossed the yard. It had been part of a playground at one time. There were lines painted on to the tarmac, partly rubbed off now.

He rounded the corner of the Hall and normality struck him like a blow. The sunshine, the people picnicking on the grass. The marquee, by the lake.

They would say today had been a great success, he knew. A coming together of village and Hope Springs. It might even become an annual event. They couldn't always guarantee this kind of weather, though.

He shuddered.

His mind was flitting from thought to thought like a butterfly, never resting, always avoiding the one thought, the memory – a snapshot image lodged in his head.

Of Jade. Of not-Jade. Her tiny bloodshot eyes, her age-worn skin, her stubs of yellow teeth. Jade, but not Jade.

Hodeken.

Danny cut through the herb garden, on to the lawn.

The first stall was the tombola. There was a great big wicker basket full of folded tickets, and all round it prizes with tickets stuck to them. Clay pots of Hope Springs honey. Giant bars of Fair Trade chocolate. Bottles of last year's perry and cider from the orchards. An envelope containing tickets for the Grafton-on-Severn cricket festival. A complete round cheese from a local farm.

'Go on,' said Sharmila from behind the stall. 'Any number ending in a five or a zero – guaranteed a prize.'

He looked at her, and saw that she was watching him with small eyes that were netted with blood vessels, talking to him through a thin-lipped mouth set in a leathery, wrinkled face.

'You know you have to,' she went on. 'Get rid of him. How can you get back to the life you want with mad Rick in the way?'

Danny turned, and walked away.

Through the crowds, he held the tray before him as if it might ward off the incubus that was haunting him.

He refused to look at anyone as he passed, but then, 'Danny, trust me,' said a woman who stood right in front of him, blocking his way. She was a large woman, with billowing black hair. She leaned towards him as she spoke and she stared at him with Hodeken's eyes, set in a plump, puffed up version of Hodeken's face.

Danny looked down, stepped round her, carried on.

From the corner of his eye, he saw someone. Sunil, he thought, watching him through his small spectacles. Watching him with Hodeken's eyes.

'It won't be long now, Danny,' he said with Hodeken's voice. 'We'll get things back to normal. You just need to do your part.'

They formed a channel for him. Straight across the lawn, a gap opened up, lined on either side by staring faces, staring eyes. Each person, as he passed, was momentarily transformed. Features distorting, twisting, lines carving themselves deep on each face in turn, hairy growths popping out across the skin, eyes breaking out in a lacework of blood vessels.

'It's okay, Danny,' said one, as he passed.

'Trust me,' said the next, acquiring Hodeken's features just as its predecessor returned to normal.

'It won't . . .'

'. . . be long now. You . . .'

'. . . just need to . . .'

'. . . do your part.'

'Get . . .'

'. . . rid . . .'

'. . . of . . .'

'. . . him.'

He threw his hands in the air and the tray went flying. The muslin cloth caught the breeze and drifted over heads like a kite, and bread rolls flew into the air like fireworks, raining down on the crowd moments later.

And the knife.

He had been carrying the knife he had spotted in the kitchen. Gripping it tightly under the tray. Bringing it with him.

He watched it shoot up, blade flashing in the sunlight. Then, at the height of its flight, it flipped, and fell to the ground, blade plunging to its hilt in the soft turf.

He stared at it, his breath snatched from his lungs.

He couldn't remember picking it up, but he knew Hodeken wanted him to have it. To be prepared.

He looked up, and they were all watching him.

He ran.

He pushed past them, through them, not caring who it was in his way, just desperate to get past them, beyond them. Away.

He came to the track into the growing plots, and Luke stood there with a garden fork held out like some kind of weapon. A small group was gathered round him, waiting for him to continue his explanation of the principles of growing vegetables by the cycles of the moon.

'Go on, Danny,' he said, in a high-pitched voice. 'Get rid of him.'

The group of onlookers nodded, as if he had simply been explaining that you should always sow peas at new moon.

Danny turned, ran on.

By the lake, David was explaining to another group how Hope Springs' waste was processed and cleansed by a sequence of reed beds.

He paused and nodded to Danny. 'Not long now, Danny,' he said through yellowed stubs of teeth. 'You just need to do your bit.'

Danny ran, his head bursting. Behind him, he could sense a babble of voices, of demands, swelling up, trying to swamp him.

He cut through the willows and came to the stream.

He hesitated, looking back, fearing that he was finally going to crack at any moment.

He took a run and jumped over the stream.

And there was silence.

The babble had cut off, just like that. The pressure ... gone.

He landed, staggering forward, and caught himself against a low stone wall.

He stopped and listened, but there was nothing.

He remembered trying to find out more about Hodeken. Searching the Internet for ways to banish him. Iron crosses and bells were said to give you some degree of protection from evil beings. As did daisy chains and ... jumping across running water!

That was what he had done.

Could he really have banished Hodeken that easily?

He doubted it. But at least it had cut off the tormenting babble, the mad sequence of images.

20

On the Cards

Can we talk? Danny Schmidt

He sat with his back against the crumbling grassy bank, and tossed small pieces of stick into the stream at his feet. He hadn't known where to go. He had to be away from Hope Springs, away from the people, and he felt safer by the moving water.

He no longer felt as if he was cracking up.

He had already cracked.

Now he just had to hold the pieces of himself together somehow.

Cassie. Whatever it was that was happening – whether it was all inside his head or not – she was the only person he knew how to talk to.

His phone buzzed.

Where? C

Slowly, he thumbed in a response.

By the stream. Where we talked family names. D

Ok. C

'Thought you'd be down at the fête, trying to convince

us yokels you're not really a bunch of devil-worshipping, sandal-wearing, bearded weirdos.'

She came and sat down next to him, her knees drawn up under her chin.

'I was, but . . .'

'What?'

'Didn't you notice anything odd?'

She looked at him, head tipped to one side, an eyebrow raised. '"Odd"? You mean *odd* odd, not just Hope Springs odd? No, nothing. What did I miss?'

He shook his head. 'Never mind,' he said. 'I think it was just me.'

'So,' she said, poking at some exposed mud with a stick. 'Let's get this straight. It's like, you phone me, you get me to make excuses to my parents so I can slip away here, halfway up this blooming great hill and find you in your little hiding place. All that, just so you can tell me not to mind, it's just you, forget about it. Have I got that right, or am I missing something, Danny Schmidt?'

He lay back and stared up at the deep blue of the sky.

'Way back,' he said. 'When . . . you said you were just normal, just a normal girl trying to make yourself sound interesting. Remember?' He paused, then added, 'Well I've worked it out. You're not normal at all. Not ordinary. You –'

'Oh-*ho*! So you don't just get me up here to tell me nothing. Oh no, you get me up here to tell me I'm abnormal! Boy, when you dig yourself a hole you dig yourself a big and a deep one, don't you? What are you going to tell me next? That I have BO and a face like a monkey's arse? Go on, Danny, keep going. I can hardly wait!'

'That's not what I meant.'

She smirked and poked her tongue out at him.

'You see inside things. That's what I mean. Or something like it. You have insight. You know a lot about . . . stuff.'

'That's not hard,' said Cassie. 'It's not special. I'm interested in things. I want to find out how the world works. How *people* work. So I find out. I look for answers. I think about things.'

'But you know the right questions to ask.'

She threw her stick towards the stream, but it got caught in some nettles. 'Maybe,' she said, 'but I can't throw straight, can I? I tell you, Danny Schmidt, you don't talk much, but when you do you sure know how to *talk*.'

She leaned back on one elbow, so that she was looking down at him, blocking out part of the blue of the sky.

'Okay,' she said. 'So you've smooth-talked me. You probably think you've wormed your way back into my good books. What now? Are you going to tell me what's going on?'

'That chat room was just the start,' he said, struggling to work out how to begin, how to explain something he didn't really understand himself. 'This sounds mad . . .'

'So do most things, when you really think about it. You and me: we're just a bunch of chemicals talking to each other. How mad is that? Go on – what's been happening?'

'Hodeken . . . he's been talking to me. Haunting my

dreams. Sitting at the back of my mind. Nagging away at me. Taunting me. That's what they do. I looked it up on the web. Kobolds taunt people, wind them up. It's been driving me mad.'

'Why? Why would he do that?'

'Some kind of pact with my family,' said Danny. 'Made in the Second World War. Maybe it even goes back beyond that and the war just stirred it up again. Hodeken sees himself as some kind of protector for the family. He won't let go.'

Danny raised an arm, and pressed his forearm across his eyes. 'He works out what needs to be done and then you have to do it for him or he drives you mad with his tricks and his taunting. I can't let that happen, Cassie. I can't let myself lose control because of a voice in my head. It happened to Dad. I have to be stronger than he was, but I don't know if I can be.'

He felt her hand on his chest, pressing softly, soothing.

'So . . . it's in your head, is it, Danny Schmidt? It's all in your head? Do you think you should get some help?'

He felt a flash of anger. Why had he thought he could talk to her? She didn't understand!

He concentrated on his breathing, but it was hard.

Eventually, he answered her.

'No,' he said. 'It's not that simple. I thought it might all be in my head until today. But at the open day he was there. Actually *there.* He took people over, one by one. Possessed them, so that their faces turned into his and they spoke with his voice. Nagging at me, taunting me.'

'What happened? What did you do, Danny?'

'I ran. I ran and I jumped over the stream to get away from them all and then suddenly it stopped. It'll be back, though. I know he won't leave me alone now.'

'How do you mean, "stopped"?'

'Everything went silent all of a sudden, as soon as I jumped the stream. I read something about it somewhere, when I was trying to find out more. I was looking for ways to get rid of Hodeken, and I came across something that told you how to ward off evil: bells, daisy chains, a self-bored stone, whatever that is – and jumping over moving water! I didn't plan it, I just did it. It was the quickest way to get away from all the madness.'

'Okay then, I've got it. You wear bells in your ears, a daisy chain in your hair and you live by a stream. That should do it.'

She had sat up as she spoke. Now she was leaning forward and poking at some loose stones.

Danny sat up, too, and watched her. 'What is it?' he asked. 'What are you doing?'

She stood and went over to the stream, then squatted to peer into the water. Squinting back at him, she said, 'You said a self-bored stone. Come on.' She beckoned to him to join her. 'Let's look for one.'

He stood and went over to the edge of the water. Kneeling in the dried mud, he stared into the swirling current. The stream bed was lined with pebbles and larger stones, some of them furred with green algae that shimmered in the flowing water.

'So?' he said. 'What am I looking for? What does it mean, a "self-bored stone"?'

Cassie had a hand in the water, rummaging through the pebbles, stirring up a swirling cloud of mud in the otherwise clear water.

'It's a stone that's been knocked about in a stream. All stones get smoothed off and worn away in the water, but a self-bored stone has a weak point somewhere in the centre and after thousands and thousands of years it ends up hollowing itself out, so you get a round stone with a hole in the middle.'

She stirred up the stones and mud again, frustrated.

Danny leaned over the water, and plucked a stone out. 'Like this?' he asked, holding it out to Cassie. On his palm, glistening wet, was a round pebble with a hole going right through it, just off-centre.

It was a curious object, but it hardly seemed like much protection from what he had been experiencing.

'How'd you do that?' demanded Cassie. She looked at the stone, and then at Danny. 'Right,' she went on. 'Now look through it.'

He held it to his right eye.

'What do you see?'

'The trees.' He turned. 'Grass. Mud. An old fence post.'

'It's supposed to be a window,' she told him. 'Into the Other World. You should see fairies dancing in the grass, that kind of thing. Maybe they're on their lunch break.'

He turned it on Cassie.

She looked scared.

Pale face, wide-open eyes . . . There was panic in those eyes, terror.

He took the stone away from his eye and she was normal, no sign of panic. She looked at him curiously. 'What?' she said. 'What is it?'

He looked at her through the self-bored stone again, and she was just Cassie, watching him and waiting. 'I . . . I don't know,' he said. 'Nothing. It's just hard to see through that small hole.'

She took it from him and looked around before eventually handing it back.

'So,' she said, 'what is it that Hodeken is after? You said he's nagging you. What about?'

He couldn't tell her. Not that much.

He blinked and saw the kitchen knife flying through the air and then plunging, right up to its handle, in the turf.

'The family,' he said. He could tell her part of it. 'He thinks he can bring the family together and we'll all live happily ever after.'

'Do you think he can?'

Danny shook his head. 'Freakish as all this stuff is,' he said, 'this isn't a fairy tale. You can't just change what's gone before. My father – he did what he did, and now he's locked away. Which is right. It's how it should be. He's a dangerous man. It terrifies me to think just how dangerous he is. You can't undo all that.

'Did I tell you he was appealing? I think that was Hodeken's doing, but it didn't work. They're not going to let him out. Hodeken's not going to get his way, but . . . but I'm scared of what he might do before he realizes that. I'm scared of what he might do to all of us.'

'I've got to go,' Cassie told him now. She had been looking at her watch as he spoke. 'I'm sorry. I told Mum I'd be back by six and it's half six already. Walk with me?'

They crossed the stream and cut along a low wall to join the lane between Moreton Farm and the village. From there they could look down the hill to where Danny had helped with the car parking that morning. Most of the vehicles had gone now. The open day must be over.

At the top of Swiss Lane, Cassie took Danny's hand and squeezed it. 'Want to come round tomorrow morning, around ten? We can ask some questions. You said I'm good at that.'

She smiled nervously, and waited for him to answer.

'Yes,' he said. 'Yes, I'd like to do that.'

She nodded. 'Got to go.'

When he was a few paces down the road, she called after him, 'Danny? One more thing. Danny – be careful. I mean that, Danny Schmidt. Be very careful.'

He carried on walking. He knew how to do that. Be careful. He'd spent all his life being careful.

It was a quiet evening, and he was thankful for that. Val and Josh stayed down at the marquee, helping clear up. Danny should have been there, too, but he couldn't face it. Not so soon. Oma was in her room, suffering from one of her bad heads, so until Val and Josh returned Danny had the place to himself.

All the time, his head was quiet and he wondered if it

really could be that straightforward; if he really had driven the kobold from his head.

He poured himself a bowl of cereal and thought about doing some of his homework, then turned the TV on for the Bond film instead.

He couldn't think straight. He couldn't follow what was happening in the film, but that didn't matter. It distracted him.

His phone vibrated against his leg. He took it out and checked the little screen: Cassie.

'So what is it, then?' she demanded, before he had a chance to say anything. 'Why now? Why can't it wait until tomorrow?'

'I . . .' He stopped, started again. 'What do you mean? Why can't *what* wait? I don't understand.'

'Your message. You texted me.'

Danny shook his head, still struggling to catch up. 'No,' he said. 'I didn't text you. I didn't do anything.' He thought for a few seconds, then added, 'This message – what number did it come from?'

'Yours, stupid. Why do you think I'm calling you?'

'Are you sure? What did it say?'

'It said, "spirit-talking – now".'

'And have you been there?'

'Think I'm stupid? Whenever I get strange requests from male admirers I always check them out first. It's a matter of principle.'

'Don't go there,' said Danny urgently. 'Do you hear? They're trying to get to you. They're trying to get at me through you. *He* is . . . Hodeken.'

'You're telling me that message wasn't from you? You're winding me up, aren't you? You have one twisted sense of humour, Danny Schmidt.'

'Just don't go there, do you hear? Don't do anything until I come in the morning, okay?' But he was talking to the connection tone. Cassie had rung off.

He took the phone away from his ear. The small screen told him he had a message from Cassie. How could she have texted him while she was on the phone to him?

He opened it.

spirit-talking – now

He called her back. 'Cassie? Trust me on this? Tell me you'll do nothing until the morning?'

'It wasn't you, was it?'

'It wasn't me. You'll leave it until the morning?'

'Until the morning.'

It was going to be another hot day. As early as he reasonably could, Danny set off down the long drive from the Hall to the main road through the village. Over on the lawn a group of people were dismantling the marquee and loading it up into an open-backed truck.

He had to get to Cassie, just to be sure she was okay. But by going to her today was he just drawing her in deeper . . . ?

He paused on the bridge over the brook and looked down at the rushing water. He needed to stop. Think. He mustn't rush into anything. He let the sound of the water soothe him, then a car swung round the bend in the road, breaking the moment. He walked on.

At the top of Swiss Lane, he hesitated again. There was the house, its bright yellow paintwork ablaze in the harsh sunlight.

He saw a face at the front window. There and then gone. She had seen him.

He went down the road and Cassie swung the door open. 'I thought you'd forgotten which house,' she said, 'you were stood there so long. I say hel-*lo*, the yellow one – remember? Hi, Dad. You remember Danny, don't you? The German kid. He was here before. I told you all about him. Hardly speaks a word of English.'

Cassie's father stood in the kitchen doorway in a dressing gown, with part of a newspaper held in one hand. 'Morning, Danny,' he said, grinning. '*Guten Morgen.*'

'Hi,' said Danny, looking from Cassie to her father and back again.

'We're going up to look on the Web, okay?' said Cassie. She stepped up on to the stairs and waved for Danny to follow.

As they went up to the landing, her father started counting off on his fingers, '*Ein. Zwei. Drei. Vier. Fünf. Sechs. Sieben . . .*'

There were three doors off the landing. One was half open into the bathroom. The one towards the front of the house was closed, and now Cassie pushed through the other into her room.

'Don't go getting any ideas,' she said to him over her shoulder. 'You can leave the door open. I know what men are like. I've read all about it.'

He followed her in, leaving the door open.

'You know what they say,' she said, turning, and spreading her hands to indicate the room's contents. 'Tidy room, tidy mind. So what did you expect?'

The room was complete chaos. Every surface was loaded with books, notepads, CD cases, clothes, plastic models of aeroplanes and monsters, magazines, pens, hair brushes, boxes . . .

'Like I say: don't go getting any ideas about tidying up or anything. Have a seat. There's one . . . over there somewhere. Pepsi?'

There was a leather cube that must be some kind of seat. He cleared the stack of magazines off it – a random mixture of *New Scientist*, *Sugar*, the *Observer Magazine* and some yellow-spined *National Geographics* – and sat, waiting.

The windows looked out over the back garden to the fields. Cassie had stuck cardboard cut-outs into the corners of the windows so that they looked like gothic arches.

'So, you going to tell me what's going on?'

'Did you get any more messages?'

She shook her head.

'It's him, Hodeken. He took over the chat room. Now he's getting to us through our phones. He can't control me, so he's trying to get to me through you now. There's one thing, I suppose: this proves it's not just in my head.'

'What? Just because I got a text message from your number? You're winding me up.'

Danny took his own phone out, thumbed the keys and handed it to Cassie. 'Did you send this message last night? It's from your number.'

She stared at it. 'God, Danny. What do we *do*?'

'You tell me to get out of here,' said Danny. 'And we hope he leaves you alone.'

'Or we stick to Plan A,' said Cassie, shaking her head. 'You came here to ask questions, so let's ask questions.'

She handed him his phone, then swept some clothes off a chair so she could sit.

She twisted in her chair so she could open up a laptop Danny hadn't noticed among all the debris on her desk. 'So what do we want to ask?'

Danny listened to the computer's mechanical chirruping as it dialled up an Internet connection.

'Okay,' said Cassie into the silence. 'You're not a morning person, are you, Danny? Hel-*lo*? Time to wake up. Okay. Here. It's remembered the search I did last time. Let's go.'

She clicked as she talked, working through a series of web pages. Danny recognized one or two of them as sites he'd found the other day.

'So, Danny.' She turned to him, and leaned forward. 'What is it that you want?'

'You're going to grant me a wish, are you?'

She snorted. 'In your dreams, matey. As if.'

'What I want? I want things to settle down again. I want to get Hodeken – whatever he or it is – out of our lives. I want it to stop interfering.'

Cassie was nodding as he spoke. 'Danny, have you asked him? Have you told Hodeken this? He's your family's guardian spirit, after all. Maybe he'd listen to you if you find the right way to ask.'

Danny started to protest, but stopped himself. Hodeken

always knew better, there was no point reasoning with the thing. But then, 'Maybe,' he told her. 'I've argued with him, over and over in my head. But I can't remember if I've actually asked him to leave us alone, just like that. I've told him that what he wants to do will never work, that it's impossible – but that's different. Maybe we just need to find the right way to persuade him to go.'

'So we need to find out how to do that. What's he like, this kobold? How would you describe him?'

Danny thought. 'Grotesque,' he said. 'Ancient. His skin's shrivelled and wrinkled and covered with lumps and little hairy warts. His teeth are yellow and they look like they've been worn down – they're too small for the spaces in his mouth. Pale eyes, with a tiny black centre and riddled with blood vessels. He wears a lumpy felt hat, pulled down hard on to his head. He hides things, and he hums tunes – he did that in a dream I had. They're the ones Oma sings. Old German tunes. I think he taught them to her.'

Cassie was clicking. 'Here's some stuff I found before. The hiding and the tunes you mentioned.'

Danny looked at the page. This was just a plain text file, no formatting. It looked like some kind of archive or transcript.

The *Hinzelmännchen* or Kobold is a small goblin-like being, who can be both a great asset to his hosts and a mischievous nuisance. Give a kobold a home in your coal cellar and he will repay you by working late into the night, finishing off chores and keeping a household in order. He is drawn to children, and will entertain them with his songs and physical humour. His favourite prank is to kick over stooping people, and

'Hang on – I'm reading.'

Cassie had been about to click the Back button.

'I dreamed this,' he told her, pointing at the screen. 'He pointed at something on the ground and I bent to pick it up and he pushed me over. When I got up he'd gone.'

he can get very angry if he is not fed properly or if he is crossed. In the 17th century, kobolds were usually depicted in paintings as little daemons with a conical hat and pointed shoes. In the class of beings from folklore, they are considered to be the most dangerous and most ugly. The *Hinzelmännchen* is drawn to extremes of emotion and takes his duties particularly seriously (even to excess, it must be said, in some legends).

Danny stared at the words, and Cassie waited patiently.

Finally, she said, 'It doesn't tell us how to get rid of him, does it? If anything, it makes it worse. It's like, don't cross them, or else!'

She set the page to print, and somewhere in the room a printer started to whine.

'Right,' said Cassie, decisively. 'He wanted us to go to Spirit Talking. Are you up for that? This might be the best way to ask him to leave you in peace.'

'I don't know.' Before, he'd been on his own in the HoST office. Now, with Cassie, it didn't seem quite so daunting. But what would Hodeken have in store for them there? 'Okay.'

The banner ad flashed up first of all, offering them genuine psychic readings at knock-down prices; then the stone-effect frame and the photograph of the smiling Dr Bob welcoming them to the site.

'Do you think they'll be there now?' Danny asked. 'Headkin or FirstLady or Lady E, or whatever they call themselves this time?'

'Who knows?' said Cassie. 'You seemed to draw them in last time. Maybe they'll show up again and you can ask them to go, if you dare.'

The link on the home page was there, as before, asking them to pick today's card. Danny nodded at it. 'What's all that about?'

Absently, Cassie clicked on the link. A playing card appeared on the screen, revealing itself from the top down. The picture was upside down. It showed a jester. The caption underneath said, '0. Fool. (INVERTED)'

'What does that mean?'

'The unknown, I think. A wild card, like a modern joker.'

'And what does it mean by "inverted"?'

'The card's been dealt upside down,' said Cassie. 'It means . . . I don't know. Deception, hidden meanings, problems. I don't like this. I've got a bad feeling about this. Let's go back and find the chat room.'

She slid the pointer across to the toolbar at the top and clicked on the Back button.

Nothing happened, then the screen flickered and the same page started to load again.

'You hit Refresh,' said Danny.

'I didn't. You saw me. I hit Back. Why's it reloading? Oh my God . . .'

A new card was revealing itself. The picture showed a stooped man in a dark cloak, carrying a long-bladed scythe. Underneath the image, the caption read, 'XIII. Death.'

Cassie clicked the 'X' in the top right corner of the window and the web browser vanished.

She turned.

'Oh, Danny,' she said. 'Oh, Danny . . .'

21

A Telephone Call and a Visit

'Call me,' Cassie urged him as she stood at the end of her drive and watched Danny leave. 'Let me know you're okay.'

'Sure,' he said, backing away, unsettled by her panicked reaction to the tarot cards. 'I'll be fine.'

Heading back to the flat, Danny realized that he was feeling frustrated. He hadn't wanted to go anywhere near that Spirit Talking website again. Not after last time and those phone messages. But today, with Cassie, it had seemed worth trying. He had psyched himself up for it, and he had been ready to go into that chat room again and confront 'Headkin'.

Maybe he would try it on his own, later.

As he walked, his thoughts kept returning to his grandmother. She knew more than she had told him. When he had asked her about Hodeken before she had played innocent, accused him of asking odd questions.

But maybe if he tried again, if he told her that he knew she and Eva and their brothers had called on Hodeken in the war, and later in East Berlin – maybe she would tell him more then.

Maybe she would tell him what her relationship with the kobold really was. She had lived with him as a presence in her life, in some form or another, for several decades, and she had not cracked like his father had. She must have worked out how to cope. She even seemed to have adapted well to his presence.

She hummed Hodeken's tunes.

And when she worked late into the night – on her own, they had always thought – just how much help did she have?

They had always thought it something of a miracle that such a frail old thing could achieve so much, but no one had objected, or queried how she did it. After the trouble with Danny's father she had just thrown herself into looking after what remained of her family and they had all accepted it gratefully.

Danny thought of all the times he had heard that familiar sound late at night. The high-pitched humming of ancient German folk tunes. How often had it been Oma, he wondered, and how often might he have listened to Hodeken humming as he worked?

Oma had the answers, but he did not know if he would be able to persuade her to share them with him.

Back at the flat, Val told him that Oma was still unwell with a bad headache. He slipped into her darkened room and was reminded of how she had been before, when Eva had been the one who fussed over people and Oma had been poorly and bedridden for much of the time.

She was an old woman, and she had suffered a lot

over recent years. Danny swallowed, and tried to stop himself from thinking along such gloomy lines.

Just then, her eyes glinted in the low light and she looked at him. 'Anthony?' she said weakly. '*Bist du es*, Anthony? Have you come back to your mother? My boy . . . is good, *ja*?

Danny backed out of the room, saying nothing. As he eased the door shut he saw that she had closed her eyes again, and appeared to be asleep.

Later, while Val prepared lunch from leftovers from the open-day catering, the phone went and Danny answered.

'Danny?'

'Yes . . .? Dad? Is that you?' Danny had been expecting his father to call at some point, as they hadn't spoken since the visit, last weekend. But he didn't usually call on a Sunday.

'Are you okay, Dad?' He had sounded odd, even in that single word, but then he had *been* odd last weekend. Losing it again.

'Danny. How are things?'

'Okay,' said Danny, sinking into the sofa in the living room. 'What's up?'

'Nothing. Nothing at all, Danny.'

Danny still couldn't put a finger on what it was that seemed so peculiar. 'Mr Peters called a couple of days ago,' he said. 'He told us about the appeal. That they didn't have enough to support it.'

'Never mind,' said his father. 'Never mind about that. It's all water under the bridge, eh?'

He was talking in a slow, measured way and suddenly Danny realized what it was that was odd: the cool, lazy way he was speaking. He had been losing it last weekend, and Mr Peters had mentioned his erratic behaviour. They were sedating him, Danny guessed. Calming him down with injections or pills.

'You sure you're okay, Dad?'

'Yeah. I'm fine, Danny. I'm cool. I've been dreaming, Danny. We could have another try, couldn't we, Danny? You're a good lad, aren't you? We can be okay . . .'

'Sure, Dad. Take it easy.'

'I will, Danny. We're cool, aren't we, Danny?'

'Yes, Dad. We're cool.'

A click, a buzz, and his father had gone.

'How would you feel if people here knew about . . . about our past?'

Danny had known something was coming. His mother had put Josh down to play in the living room once he had finished his lunch and for the last few minutes she had sat toying with her food, barely eating a thing.

'I don't know,' said Danny. 'It'd be tough. But it'd be a relief, too, in some ways. Why?'

'We can't hide it away forever,' she said. 'If the appeal had gone through it would have been in the papers again. Someone would have made the connection. I think . . . well, it's bound to happen at some stage.'

He cracked open one of the rolls, and pulled at its soft insides. 'That might be a good thing,' he said. He wasn't as sure as he sounded. The thought of what he had been through before! But they couldn't keep running and hiding forever.

'There's a chance it might come out soon,' Val told him. She was talking slowly, as if choosing her words with great care. 'Someone knows already.'

'Rick?'

She looked up at him, sharply. 'How . . .?'

'He told me,' said Danny. 'I assumed you must have told him.'

'He was being inquisitive, pushy. I thought I was being clever. I wanted to put him off, so I said your father was a violent man, a jealous man. I thought that might scare Rick off.'

'Scare him off? You mean . . .' Danny wasn't sure *what* she meant.

'Rick's very single-minded,' said Val. 'He isn't easily put off. He went away and dug up our past, and now he's threatening me. I don't want to lose what we have, Danny. I don't know what to do.'

'How's he threatening you? Why?'

'Because he loves me, he claims. He's convinced that he's going to win me over, and that anything is forgivable in the long run. I should feel flattered, I suppose. You read about people like him: people so fixated that they can't see how things really are. For some people it's some kind of medical condition – an illness. And now he's casually mentioning how awful life would be for you if word got out about our past. How difficult it would be at school. He keeps telling me how he's in a position where he can protect you. But by putting it like that he's also making it absolutely clear that he can make life hell for you, too.'

She was crying now, and Danny sat silently for a time. 'He said that to me, too,' he said finally.

She looked up, surprised.

'He said he could make life hell for you, too, if I didn't keep out of it. He's been threatening both of us, Mum.'

Another drawn-out silence.

'Do you want to be rid of him?' Danny asked softly.

He remembered the lump of rock in his hand, that night he had followed them.

And the knife, flying through the air, burying itself in the soft ground.

He knew what Hodeken would have him do to get Rick out of the way . . .

Val nodded. 'There's nothing I'd like more,' she said.

'Then tell him to go,' Danny said. 'Tell him to leave us all alone.'

Before anything worse happens.

But by that stage, things were out of Danny's control.

Early that afternoon, he took Josh down to the lawn by the lake.

'Tent?' said the little boy, wandering round in circles where the marquee had been. 'Want big tent!'

'You're in it,' said Danny. 'Can't you see it?'

Josh stopped and looked all around, and then at Danny. 'Liar,' he said. 'Pants on fire, liar.'

He trotted off towards the water, where bees hummed over the clover and, out over the lake, swallows darted and skimmed low across the surface. 'Don't go too near the edge,' said Danny, hurrying after him.

He wondered how Val was getting on. She had gone to find Rick. To reason with him, she said. To convince him that he was wasting his time.

The sunny weather had shifted slightly. The air was muggy, thick. It felt as if it was pressing in on Danny. There was sweat on his forehead, even though he had only been walking slowly. Over in the west, the sky's blue butted up against a thick grey wall of cloud. A storm was coming.

He thought of Cassie as, he realized, he often thought of her. She had asked him to call her, tell her he was okay.

He reached into his pocket for the phone, then stopped. He could always call her later. Right now, Josh had headed off on the trail through the willows, and Danny hurried to catch up with him.

Later, they came up through the orchard.

When he spotted Rick working among the trees, Danny considered turning back, but it was too late. Rick waved, wiping his forehead with a small white cloth. He seemed relaxed, as if nothing had happened. Maybe Val hadn't found him after all.

'Danny. Josh,' he said as they approached. He was standing by a neat stack of logs, all cut to a length of about thirty centimetres and split neatly into quarters. Where he had been working, there was another log, standing on end, with a small hand axe embedded in it and a mallet and wooden wedges arranged nearby.

Josh ran up to him and started making buzzing noises

as he ran in tight circles round the teacher's legs. 'Hey there!' cried Rick. He lifted Josh with a hand under each armpit and spun him round in the air.

After a short time, he put the boy down and laughed at him while he staggered around trying to regain his balance.

Then he looked sideways at Danny. 'I spoke to Val,' he said.

Danny looked at him, but couldn't work out his expression.

'She seemed confused,' Rick continued. 'Over-emotional, I'd say. Has she been okay lately?'

This was man-to-man stuff. Consulting Danny about woman trouble.

'Some of the things she was saying, Danny. As I say – very confused. I think I see your hand in that. Would I be right?' Still smiling, still talking casually, good mates having a chat. 'Don't you remember our little conversation, Danny? I thought we understood each other.'

He took out his cloth again, unfolded it, and dabbed at his brow, then folded it and put it away again. He stooped, took the axe in one hand and the mallet in the other. He tapped at the small log and it fell from the axe's blade.

'I'm disappointed in you, Danny,' Rick continued. 'You know what I'd like? I have this . . . I suppose you'd call it a vision, a daydream. What I'd like is, when Val and I are together, I'd like to be able to treat you and Josh, here, like my own sons. We'd do things together. You'd have a father figure to look up to. How about that?'

He swung the axe down, and it stuck deep in the log. He hammered it deeper with the mallet until the log split in two.

'I don't want us to be enemies, Danny.' He took one half of the log, turned it through ninety degrees and swung the axe down again to split it.

'And I don't think you'd want that, either, would you?'

They followed the path round the corner of the Hall. Danny carried Josh, the little boy tired and cross with the sticky heat.

Danny was nervous. He wondered what state Val might be in now. She had quite clearly failed to get through to Rick.

They emerged in a gap between an ancient yew tree and the corner of the main building. As usual, for a weekend, the car park was pretty much full with the hostas' cars. HoST was running fewer residential courses this weekend because of the open day, but there were still at least three groups that Danny was aware of.

There was a car pulled up across the drive, though, as if the driver had tried to park, found no spaces and just pulled up where he could.

Standing by the car, in the shade of the lime trees, was a policeman.

Danny's heart rushed, suddenly. For him, the sight of that uniform would always be an alarming thing.

He turned, and there was Val, talking to a man and a woman by the door to the flat. They were clearly police, even though they were not in uniform. There was something about them, something Danny had learned to spot.

Josh squirmed in his arms, and Danny relaxed his grip, allowing the little boy to slide down, wriggle free and run across the gravel to his mother.

Danny followed, more slowly.

He studied her face as she spoke, paused, glanced across at him, and then carried on speaking.

She was pale, her movements jerky, nervous.

Josh reached her and threw his arms round her legs. He knew when things weren't right.

'... but how?' she insisted, as Danny drew near. 'How *could* he?' She turned to Danny and explained, 'It's your father, Danny. They say ... they say he's got out.'

She was speaking very slowly, as if she still couldn't believe what she had been told. 'Somehow,' she said, 'he just managed to walk out of there.'

Danny looked at the two police officers. One, a dark-haired woman in her thirties carefully avoided his look. The older one, a man with a bristly grey moustache and a weary look in his eye, said, 'He didn't just walk out, Mrs Smith. It's not quite clear how it happened. Nothing like it has ever happened there before. There was a lot of confusion. Somehow he managed to talk his way through to the outer gates before anyone challenged him. That guard is in intensive care now.' The officer looked away. He looked embarrassed.

His colleague spoke up now. 'As I was saying, Mrs Smith ... Have you or your family had any contact with your husband since Danny and his grandmother visited last Saturday?'

'He called,' said Danny. They all looked at him. 'Today. At lunchtime – about oneish. He seemed odd. Spaced out. When did he escape?'

The two officers were staring at him.

'He broke out this morning, shortly after eleven,' said the man. 'What did he say? Did he tell you where he was?'

Danny shook his head. 'Nothing,' he said. 'He wasn't on the phone for long. He asked how we were. Said he'd been dreaming.'

'Did he mention anyone else?'

Danny looked at the officer, confused. 'Who?' he asked. 'Why would he mention anyone else?'

'There were reports from the prison,' said the officer, 'that when he escaped there may have been another individual involved. A small man. Very old. Wearing an odd hat.'

Hodeken.

No wonder Danny's head had been relatively quiet today. His tormentor had been busy elsewhere.

22

A Dark and Stormy Night

They all sat in the living room. The TV was on. Celebrities doing something dumb for Bank Holiday entertainment. Danny wasn't really following it.

Val sat on the sofa, her feet tucked up under her, a gin and tonic cradled in both hands. Josh sat on the floor, scribbling in a colouring-in book. He hadn't quite grasped the idea of colouring in the right places yet. He should have been in bed by now, but Val seemed content to let him play.

By the window, Oma Schmidt stood, as she had stood for the past two hours. She stared out through the glass, peering into the gathering dusk.

Waiting.

What had Hodeken told her, Danny wondered.

There was a clatter of crockery from the kitchen. No household sprite, this was Detective Constable Fox making herself useful and keeping out of the way.

'We have no reason to expect him to come here,' Fox's superior, Detective Inspector Lever, had assured Val earlier. 'It's far more likely with cases like this . . .' Not that there *were* cases like this. '. . . that the absconder would return to somewhere familiar. His childhood haunts in Eastbourne, maybe, or back to your old home in Loughton, or maybe to where . . . to the scene of his crimes. No, there's nothing to indicate that he would want to come here.'

Nothing, that is, apart from the phone call he had made at lunchtime, two hours after he had escaped. That, and Oma Schmidt standing by the window, watching and waiting.

The other possibility, Lever had told them, was that Danny's father might just try to vanish: sleeping rough, living in homeless shelters where no one need know who he was. That was a possibility they might have to learn to live with: the knowledge that he may be out there somewhere, hiding. No one would know where he was. No one would know when he might, finally, decide to pay them a visit . . .

Rain blasted the window in a sudden, furious flurry. Still Oma stood there, watching.

The room was lit by a tall lamp standing in the corner, and the flickering, dancing colours of the television. Danny stood, and went over to turn on the main light.

'Daddy,' said Josh, looking up.

Danny, standing in the doorway, turned sharply.

The landing was empty. Josh hadn't seen anything. He might just have said 'Danny', after all.

'No,' said Danny, walking over to him and squatting by the boy. 'Your daddy is dead, Josh. Your daddy died three years ago.'

He was killed by *my* daddy in a jealous rage, fuelled by the taunting voices that filled his head.

He looked up at Val. She hadn't reacted. She wasn't going to deny it. It was the first time this unspoken truth had been brought out into the open. Josh was Chris Waller's son, from the affair Val had been having with the man who was her husband's best friend.

Josh was scribbling again. He had been on that page for hours.

'Have you got homework, Danny?' asked Val.

'I'll look.' He had no idea. School seemed so far away, right now. He went out to the landing, went to peer down into the stairwell. The door at the bottom was locked now, and there were policemen in a car out in the car park.

He went to his bedroom and switched on the light. The room was empty.

He kneeled by the bed and pulled the box out. He emptied the envelope on to his duvet. The photos, the newspaper cuttings.

He stared at them without picking them up.

He didn't need reminding of anything.

He gathered them up and stuffed them into the envelope, which he then folded in two and twisted tightly. He dropped it in his bin.

He went back into the living room and stood by Oma.

It was dark now, and the window was streaked with rain. Lightning flickered and rumbled in the distance. There was a light in one of the cars, the faint orange glow of a cigarette. It flared bright as its owner inhaled, and then faded. A few seconds later it glowed bright again.

'Is he out there, Oma?' asked Danny.

She looked at him. 'How should I know?' she asked him. 'I am only an old woman. All I see is rain and the dark.'

But she was smiling as she spoke.

The phone buzzed in his pocket. He took it out and looked at the small screen. He had a message.

U sed youd call but hvnt. WHY?! RU OK? C

What to tell her? His psychopathic father had nearly killed a guard, escaped from prison and might just be outside now. Oh yes, and he has the help of a mad, obsessive creature from German legend.

No. Best to keep it simple, he thought.

Sorry. Forgot. All ok. You ok? DS

Just then, there was a crackle of someone's voice from DC Fox's radio in the kitchen. Danny stood and arched his back to get rid of some of the stiffness.

Oma had retreated from the window to an armchair where she sat quietly, eyes still open, watching. Val sat on the sofa with Josh's head in her lap, the little boy stretched out on the sofa, fast asleep.

Outside, lightning still danced in the distance.

Danny went through to the landing, paused to peer down the stairs at the locked front door, and then went to stand in the kitchen doorway.

DC Fox sat at the table with a mug of tea, looking at one of Val's alternative lifestyle magazines. She looked up at Danny.

'All quiet in there?' she said, through a professional smile.

Danny nodded. 'Any news?' he asked her.

'No, nothing. Sorry.'

Danny's phone buzzed, but he ignored it for now.

'He'll come here,' he said. 'Why else would he have phoned after he'd got out? He'll hitch a lift, or he'll sneak a free ride on a train, or if it comes to it, he'll just walk, but however he does it he'll come here.'

'Go to sleep, Danny. It's late. We're here to protect you, and to catch him.'

'The prison guards were there to keep him in prison, but they couldn't stop him, could they?'

He turned and went back to the living room. He went to the window where Oma had stood for much of the evening. He checked his phone.

Fine here. Nite nite Danny Schmidt. C xx

The day broke, bright and hot. Danny sat in his room's window seat and watched the steam rising from puddles in the car park below.

He had slept little, but he felt strangely rested. Sharmila's breathing exercises helped – there were benefits to living in a place like Hope Springs.

Two plain-clothes officers were in a car below. Danny couldn't quite work out whether their strategy was to be visible in order to scare his father off, or to be hiding so that they could pounce on him when he marched up to the front door.

He surveyed the trees.

His father was used to hiding and watching.

Nothing.

As the sun rose, the ground dried. Soon you would be hard put to tell it had rained at all last night.

Danny took his phone out and reread Cassie's last message. He keyed out a new one for her.

Things happening. U should stay away from here 2day. CU tomorrow. DS.

He looked at his watch. Six thirty in the morning. It was going to be a long day.

It was the church bells that set her off, ringing in the hour at ten in the morning.

'But you haven't been to church in years,' said Val, exasperated by her mother-in-law's sudden, odd request.

Oma stood on the landing, her arms folded. 'My boy is in trouble,' she said. 'I want to pray for him.'

Pray to whom? Danny wondered. Or to what ancient god?

'The church will probably be locked,' said Val, stubbornly. 'They do that these days. How are we going to get you there? You can hardly walk all that way. Can't you just pray here?'

'I want to go to church.'

'There's the old school chapel,' said Danny.

Val glanced at him. He wasn't sure if she was irritated or grateful at his intervention. The school chapel was attached to the east wing of Wishbourne Hall. It had been locked up and unused for years, but more recently, as HoST had started to offer more courses for its weekend visitors, the pews had been removed and the chapel had been used as a hall for yoga and meditation sessions.

A short time later, Danny stood with DC Fox at the top of the stairs. 'Give us five minutes,' he told his mother. 'I'll call to let you know it's okay.'

She nodded, and he went down the stairs after the officer.

Outside, the air had that freshness of rain after heat, as if the world had been reborn. Danny waited while DC Fox spoke to her colleagues in the car.

Danny rubbed at his tired eyes and waited.

Then he turned and she was there, standing right in front of him. Cassie. Her dark hair was almost purple in the morning's harsh sunlight.

'I said –'

'I know,' she interrupted. 'So what is it? What's so awful that you tell me to stay away, and that there's a police car parked down at the entrance to the Hall and them here?' She nodded at the unmarked police car as she spoke.

'My dad,' said Danny. 'He's escaped from prison.' He glanced at the police officers, and then added, 'Hodeken helped him.'

'Oh God, Danny. I knew something was happening. Something bad. I could feel it.'

'Who's this?' said DC Fox, joining them.

'A friend,' said Danny. 'Cassie. Let's go.'

The three threaded their way through the parked cars and then followed the path across in front of the Hall to the far wing. As they walked, Danny explained to Cassie about Oma's sudden insistence that she should be allowed to pray.

Round the corner, they could look out across the lawn to the lake. Someone was down there, riding the mower back and forth across the grass.

Danny produced the heavy key Val had given him and unlocked the wooden door into the chapel. Light flooded in through the doorway and the tall windows. The walls had been whitewashed and in this light they shone glaringly.

Chairs were stacked against one wall, but otherwise the main area was empty. DC Fox went through to the annexe, where there was a small kitchen and some storage space.

'Nothing,' she said, coming out moments later. 'I think we can safely give the all-clear.'

Cassie went to get some of the chairs down. 'Might as well have somewhere to sit,' she said brightly.

Danny took his phone from his pocket and speed-dialled the flat's number. 'Val? Danny. It's okay. You can come over now.' Then he added, 'I've got a friend with me. Cassie. It's okay, she knows about all this.'

DC Fox was in the doorway. 'Back in a minute,' she said.

Danny went to the door, and watched her head back round the building. He looked down across the lawn again. The mower was still moving from side to side of the wide green area. The air shimmered with heat haze.

He heard a voice. Rick. Laughing and talking. Danny

sighed. The last thing they wanted was Rick interfering right now.

More voices, to his right. Danny looked, and saw DC Fox leading Val, Josh and the shuffling Oma round the side of the Hall.

Danny leaned against the door frame, suddenly dizzy. The voices, drawing in from all sides . . . He struggled to piece it all together.

Who was Rick talking to?

He looked along the paved path that led through a narrow rose bed to the steps at the top of the lawn.

Rick was approaching, looking back down the steps. He was still laughing and talking. He was a popular man, after all. People *liked* Little Rick.

To the right, DC Fox, Val and Oma approached, Josh toddling around merrily at their feet.

'Val? Yes. You know, I'm really lucky there. She's a fine woman. I couldn't be luckier, could I, Danny? Danny! Isn't that right? Me and your mum?'

But Danny was staring at the man who followed Rick up the steps and now across the path through the roses. The man was smiling, nodding, agreeing with Rick, one hand on his companion's arm, the other behind his own back.

As the man half turned, Danny saw that something part wood and part metal was hooked into the back of his trousers.

'Hey, Danny, what are you doing in the chapel?' said Rick. Just at that instant, he seemed to sense something. A hint of strangeness. A tension. A suggestion that, even though the day was sunny and the woman he loved was now standing nearby ... despite all this, just the faintest suggestion that all was not, in fact, right with the world.

Danny saw this crossing his teacher's mind, in the briefest flicker of confusion.

'This chap,' Rick said, faltering, trying to pick up his momentum again, 'he says he knows you, Danny. He ...'

'He's my father.'

Rick stopped, turned his head, stared.

Danny's father smiled and nodded. 'You were saying?'

And with his free hand, he pulled something from the back of his trousers. It was the hand axe Rick had been using to split logs the previous day.

The blade was a dull grey, all apart from the cutting edge which glinted now in the sunlight. These tools have to be kept sharp if they are to be any good. Rick was very careful about such things. Blunt tools are dangerous.

But then, sharp tools can be dangerous, too.

A sudden movement.

So fast! Like a snake striking.

The hand that had been on Rick's arm shot upwards and grabbed him by his ponytail. It yanked down, so that his neck was exposed to the sunlight.

'I think you were telling me about my wife,' said Danny's father, still in that slow, lazy tone he had used on the phone the previous lunchtime. He held the axe poised at about shoulder height. Ready to swing it down on to Little Rick's neck.

Danny stepped towards the two of them. 'Let him go, Dad,' he said softly. He could see the tendons stretched tight in Rick's neck, his Adam's apple bobbing as he tried to swallow.

'Danny?' His father stared at him, squinting a little.

'Yes, Dad. It's me. Let Rick go. We can talk.'

DC Fox was at Danny's elbow now. 'Mr Smith,' she said. 'Drop the axe and release this man. I'm a police officer and I'm not alone. Give yourself up now. It's all over.'

Danny's father still smiled. 'I can do what I want,' he said. 'I can walk right through your lot and you won't bat an eyelid.'

Fox faltered, and that was when Rick spotted his chance.

'Hey!' he called. 'Hey, Josh! Look who's here. It's your daddy. Josh, come and see your daddy.'

Danny stared at him, horrified, and then, following a movement of Rick's and his father's eyes he turned.

Josh darted away from Val and Oma and ran across the paved area, chuckling away as he did so. 'Daddy?' he called. 'Daddy?'

Danny's father stared down at the little red-haired boy.

Rick swung an arm up and batted the axe away, then ducked, twisted, and pulled himself free. Staggering, turning, he backed away, stumbling on the path. 'I . . .' he croaked. 'I . . .' He looked round the small gathering, then turned and sprinted away.

'Daddy?'

Danny's father stooped, holding an arm out to the little boy. Josh went to him, still chuckling away, waving a little hand as he was swept up off the ground.

Please don't let him work out who Josh actually is, Danny thought.

DC Fox took a step closer. A step too close.

In a single movement, Danny's father straightened with Josh held in the crook of his arm, and with his other hand he swung the axe upwards, straightening his arm, extending his reach.

Danny flinched as the axe made contact. The soft thud it made against the police officer's face would be with him forever. The faint, surprised gasp as she fell back, and then slumped to one side into the roses.

It was over in an instant, and it was only in the long seconds afterwards that Danny saw DC Fox move a little after landing, saw the rise and fall of one shoulder as she breathed and he knew that, for now at least, she lived. It was only then that he made sense of what he had seen: the blade, pointing the wrong way so that the blunt end had struck the officer, not the finely honed cutting edge.

And now: a piercing wail burst out from Josh.

'So . . .' said Danny's father, holding Josh high on his left arm as the toddler squirmed and cried. 'Who are you, then, young man?'

'Put him down, Tony.' This was Val, standing with Oma by the chapel door. As Danny looked up at her, he saw Cassie hiding inside.

'Put him down, Dad,' he said. 'It's over. Rick will have *phoned the police* by now.' He doubted that, but he did hope that his emphasis on those words might prompt Cassie into phoning for help, if she hadn't already.

'Val?' said his father, now. Josh was making a choked

sobbing sound, looking from adult to adult, confused. 'Is that you, Val? Am I dreaming again? It always seems so . . . real. Val, I've come for you, and for my little boy. Val, we'll go away. Start all over again. We'll be a happy family. You just need to give me a chance.'

'Put him down, Dad. Will you put the little boy down?'

'You . . .' His father's expression changed now. His eyes narrowed, his skin became more flushed. He squinted at the axe as he raised it again. There was blood on the blade from where he had struck DC Fox.

'You keep talking to me,' he said. 'My head.'

'It's me, Dad. Danny. Your son. Put the little boy down.'

His father shook his head.

Josh was growing frustrated. He twisted and called, 'Mummy? Danny?'

Just then, Oma slumped against the wall and Val caught her, held her, guided her so that she sat down slowly instead of falling.

'I'll have your tongue,' Danny's father told him now. 'Just like the others.' He shook his head again, as if trying to dislodge something.

'Do it then,' said Danny. 'But you'll have to put the boy down first.' He put his hands out, as if to take Josh.

The boy wriggled and Danny's father eased his grip enough for him to twist free and run to his mother.

'It's okay, Dad. It's all over. It's Danny. You know who I am, don't you?'

'The voices . . .'

'I know. In your head. Hodeken. I know about him, Dad. I know all about him. He's real. He's tormenting you. Don't let him, Dad. Stand up to him.'

Just then, Danny was aware of a flickering in the corner of his vision, something flashing through the rose bed.

A small figure. A little man with a pointed hat.

'You can beat him, Dad.'

And Hodeken stood by his father's side. 'It's no good, Danny. That's the trouble. Can't you see? He hears me but he doesn't believe. He won't let himself see me. Here I am, trying to help, and he just can't let himself see!'

Danny glared at the little figure, its twisted, gnarled old features, its eyes that claimed to understand but didn't really understand a thing.

'Go away!' he snapped. 'Leave us alone. We don't want you. We don't want you interfering and making a mess of our lives. You're not needed – can't you see?'

Hodeken stared at him.

'Just leave us alone. We don't need you.'

His father grunted, snatching Danny's attention away from the kobold.

He had raised the axe.

He was staring at Danny, pure madness in his eyes.

'Oh yes, you do,' chirped Hodeken.

He jumped up and slapped Danny's father on the cheek. When the man looked down, he seemed to see something on the path and he stooped for a closer look.

Hodeken darted round behind him, sprang into the air and gave him an almighty two-footed kick in the seat of his trousers.

Danny's father went sprawling on the paving slabs and Danny leaped on top of him.

The axe . . . it had slipped from his father's grip. In the instant Danny saw it lying on the path, he reached for it, found the base of its handle and managed to flip it over, beyond their reach.

Winded by the fall, his father gasped for air, but then with frightening strength he swung an arm, catching Danny in the side with his elbow.

He swung again, and then bucked his body and almost managed to throw Danny clear.

Danny hung on, desperate. It could only be seconds before he was toppled, and then his father would do whatever it was he wanted to do.

Then there were hands on his back, and legs and feet in the corner of his vision.

Someone pulled at him, and someone kicked him in the hip, sending a bolt of pain the length of his body.

He fell back, clear, and an elbow or a knee caught him in the face. He ducked his head and struggled out from the pile of fighting men.

Lying on his side, he looked back and saw policemen, three or maybe four of them, pinning his father to the ground. He slumped back, almost blacking out with the pain in his side and his head.

He felt a hand on his chest, gentler this time.

Cassie.

'You never told me you were a bloody hero,' she said, and flung her arms round him, sobbing.

23
Hinzelmännchen

They made Hodeken bread. They borrowed the recipe, the strong organic flour and the yeast from Jade. They mixed the ingredients and kneaded the dough, taking it in turns to press and fold, to knock it back and knead again.

As they left the bread to bake, they sat in the window seat in Danny's room. Outside, the sun was low, the light magical and golden through the trees.

'So what did you see?' Danny asked her.

'I saw what happened,' Cassie told him. 'I saw you arguing with your father, persuading him to let Josh go after he had knocked out the policewoman. I saw him . . . I saw the way he swung the axe up high and he was about to swing it down . . . at *you*, Danny. And then as he swung, you sidestepped him, or ducked, or something. It wasn't clear. It was so fast. And he went flying over you and you were on him and holding him down until the police came.'

When the timer rang out, they went back to the kitchen and took the bread from the oven.

'So,' said Cassie. 'Are you going to tell me what this is all about?'

Danny went to the fridge and took out a carton of milk. 'We're going to say goodbye to Hodeken,' he said. 'I've been thinking through some of the stuff we found, and some of the things Hodeken has shown me. He's devoted himself to my family for half a century, probably far longer. Despite all the harm he's caused, he's protected us when he could. I think we should recognize that. Without Hodeken, Oma and her sister and brothers probably wouldn't have survived the war.'

He poured the milk into a simple china cup. 'When Eva called to him during the war, they had to ask him three times in succession and they made him an offering. Kobolds like the simple things, plain food like bread and milk. They don't like complications. I think our world is too complex for him. He's trying to do his best but he just doesn't get it. I think that if we ask him in the right way we might get through to him. Eva managed it, all those years ago: we just need to do it the way she did.'

'So are you going to tell me where he's hiding?'

Danny tore the loaf in half and put one piece on a plate. He took it with the cup of milk and nodded for Cassie to follow. He remembered Oma pushing over Luke so that he fell into the flowers and then running away like a schoolgirl. He remembered how ill she had been, but how she had recovered after Eva's death and taken to looking after what remained of her family, how fiercely she tried to keep things together.

Across the landing, he paused before Oma's bedroom door, knocked with the toe of his shoe and entered.

She lay in the darkened room, her blanket pulled up to

her nose. When he entered, Danny saw the briefest of flickers as she closed her eyes, pretending to be asleep.

'Hodeken?' he said gently. 'We've brought you supper. This is Cassie, my friend. I think you'll like her.'

Oma didn't move.

Danny put the plate and cup on the chest of drawers by her bed, and perched himself on the edge of the mattress.

He remembered those last images from his dream of Berlin. Great-Aunt Eva hurrying to pack, shortly before the knock came on her door from the state security police. Eva, slumped against the wall, hugging Hodeken and then, in the blink of an eye, the kobold was gone and she was hugging herself.

All the time he had been with them, he had hidden in the most secure place of all.

He had hidden within.

Danny took the self-bored stone from his pocket and held it to his eye. Before him, the shape of his grandmother flickered, as if it were only weakly held together.

And there – a form that at first he could only vaguely make out but which grew steadily stronger, he saw the little man. *Hinzelmännchen.* Staring warily back at him.

'Hodeken,' said Danny. 'It's time to leave.'

'You said you didn't want me,' said the nasal voice. 'You said you didn't need me, but you did, didn't you?'

Danny had been right. Hodeken had retreated to his hiding place, and he was sulking.

'We didn't need you,' said Danny. 'You were only putting right a situation you had created.'

'I was only doing my best,' said the little man. 'I was

only trying to make your dream come true. Is that such a bad thing to try to do?'

'No,' said Danny. 'It's a very noble thing to do. We appreciate all that you have done for us in the past, but we don't need your protection any more. It's a big and complicated world out there and you are out of your time. We have other ways of dealing with things now. You just make things worse when you get involved.'

'You're not cross with me?'

Danny thought. This creature had wrecked his family, destroyed his father. 'I'm sad,' said Danny. 'Very sad. You meant well, but you've done so much harm . . . caused so much pain. Do you see what you've done to us?'

He had to stop. This was all so painful.

A short time later, he continued. 'I just wish I'd understood sooner. But I was so wrapped up in my own little world that I didn't see what was happening. I've spent the last three years being so terrified that I would turn out like my father that I've forgotten to try to turn out like *myself*.'

He turned to Cassie then, and took her hand. 'The poem's right: our parents do mess us up, but we mess ourselves up, too.'

'It's been hard,' said Hodeken. 'Maybe I could have a rest . . .'

'Just one thing,' said Danny. 'Would you do us one final favour before you leave?'

Hodeken's face lit up. He smiled. He winked. He said, 'Close your eyes and make your wish, and I'll do my best. As long as it's not too complicated!'

Danny closed his eyes and wished.

After a short time, he opened them again.

'You're really going to be okay?' said the small voice.

'Yes, I am. We are.'

'Truly?' he asked again.

'Yes.'

'You don't need me?'

At the third time of asking, Danny hesitated and then he nodded.

He lowered the self-bored stone and studied his grandmother's face. For a few more seconds she breathed peacefully, and then there was a rattle in her throat, a half-cough, and she stopped.

Cassie gasped, and Danny squeezed her hand. He had hoped and hoped that it wouldn't happen like this, but he had suspected that it would. He swallowed. He had lost so much.

'Hodeken's been keeping her going for three years,' he said. 'If he goes, she goes, too.' When Eva had died, the kobold must have moved his attentions to her sister, which explained why she had suddenly roused herself from her various illnesses and rallied in the face of adversity to look after what was left of her family.

He looked at his grandmother again through the hole in the stone, but all he saw was a little old woman, lying in her bed, not moving, not breathing, not *being*.

24

Normal Again

Cassie came the next morning. They had breakfast with Val and then Danny and Cassie gathered up Josh so that they could take him out to leave Val free to make arrangements for Oma Schmidt's funeral.

'You will call Christian and Dieter, won't you?' Danny had asked earlier. Val had nodded and assured him that she would. For Oma's sake. And who knows? Maybe, after all this, Oma's brothers would respond and the family would start to pull together again.

'What a way to spend your half-term,' Val said as Danny, Cassie and Josh left. 'All this . . .'

'It's a first for me,' said Cassie.

Danny led her down the stairs by the hand, aware of his mother watching and realizing that it only bothered him a bit.

'Have you heard anything about your dad?' asked Cassie as Josh ran off across the grass ahead of them.

Danny shook his head. 'I think they've got him locked up as safely as they possibly can, just to be sure. It'll sort itself out. He'll be moved to another prison and I'll be able to start visiting him again – I'll find an adult to accompany me. They won't let me go on my own. It'll all be back to normal before we know it.'

'Normal,' said Cassie, and grunted.

'Yes, "normal",' said Danny. 'Whatever that is.'

They walked around the grounds, following a path that took them through the trees to the orchard, and there they saw Little Rick. He had his beekeeper's gear on and was puffing smoke into one of his hives to pacify the bees.

Josh ran up to him and started running round in circles making buzzing sounds.

Rick straightened, took his hat off and beamed at them.

'Hey, Danny! Cassie! How are things today after our little bit of excitement? I was going to call in later. I heard about Omaschmidt.'

Danny looked at him, and then at Cassie whose face had gone purple and looked just about ready to explode. He grinned at her, and watched her expression shift from outrage to puzzlement.

'You're not welcome here,' said Danny to Rick. 'I want you to leave us alone. Me. Val. All of us.'

Rick was still smiling, but with less confidence now.

Behind him, the buzzing had grown just a little more persistent, just a little louder, as first one or two, and then a growing mass of bees gathered on top of the hive.

It was stupid to hope that things could ever be perfect. Life had its ups and its downs and you just had to cope. But it didn't seem such a bad thing to hope for a few more ups than downs. It might just start to balance out all the low points they had endured.

And life at Hope Springs could be pretty good for them if they were only given a chance. A bit of peace.

It didn't seem too much to wish for.

Rick was uncomfortable now. Looking around. He knew something was up, but he hadn't quite worked out what it was yet.

Danny stepped back, pulling Cassie with him. 'Josh?' he called. 'Over here, Josh.'

A great big lump of bees broke away from the top of the hive and flew straight up in the air. They hung there for what seemed like forever as more and yet more flew up to join them.

Rick looked up at them. He had probably never seen anything like this before. He looked worried.

He had good reason to be worried.

The swarm dropped, plunging through the air.

Rick made a strangled yelping sound, and darted out of their way.

The swarm swooped low over the ground and then swung back up into the air again.

Rick looked at it, and then at Danny, and then he began to run.

The bees followed him and dived down, and he ducked and tripped and sprawled in the mud. He scrambled to his feet again and ran, and soon he was lost from sight.

That was the last that was ever seen of Little Rick at Hope Springs. Nobody ever did explain why he had just gone off, never to return. He was so popular and liked by everyone, after all. And nobody could explain, either, why every last one of his beehives had been abandoned from that day onwards, too.

Only Danny knew, but he didn't tell anyone. Wishes should be secret things and they should not be shared with anyone if you want them to come true, and if you want them to stay true.

Danny woke and washed and dressed and shoved today's books into his school bag. It was June now and they were well into the second half of the summer term. Already, Danny was looking forward to the long summer holiday.

He looped the ready-knotted tie over his head and tightened it. His blazer was still too small, but it should see out the term.

He went through to the kitchen and made himself coffee and toast. 'You okay?' asked Val, looking up from her notes.

He nodded. Yes, he was, he realized. He was okay.

Outside, the usual group was heading for school, a short distance ahead. He quickened his stride to catch up with them.

'Hi, everyone,' he said to Jade, Won't and Tim as he joined them.

He listened to the two brothers, arguing about cricket again. Partway round the village, Won't turned to Danny and said, 'You coming to the cricket on Saturday? It's the Grafton-on-Severn festival.'

Danny shook his head. 'No,' he said. 'I'm going to visit my dad on Saturday.' David and Sharmila were taking him. This would be his first visit since Oma had died.

They'd spoken on the phone a few times, though, and Danny's father seemed calmer now, more settled since Hodeken had gone.

'Ha! Makes a change from him coming to visit *you*, doesn't it?' Won't laughed, dodging out of the way of Danny's bag as it swung towards his head.

Danny laughed, too, gathering up his bag again. 'Yes,' he said. 'I think this is the best way round, all in all.'

Ahead of them, Cassie was waiting with Jo Lee at the start of the track. Danny found himself grinning. A stupid, dumb grin which he just couldn't get off his face.

Nick Gifford

The Facts

Place and date of birth:
Dovercourt, Essex, 1966

Favourite book:
So many! John Wyndham's The Day of the Triffids, F. Scott Fitzgerald's The Great Gatsby and Robert Silverberg's Dying Inside.

Most treasured possession:
Photos of my children when they were younger and the computer back-ups for my work – most other things can be replaced.

Photograph © Pete Millson

Favourite song:
Current favourites include almost anything by the Libertines, They Might Be Giants, The Colorblind James Experience or the Beatles.

Favourite film:
Pulp Fiction or When Harry Met Sally.

Favourite memory:
The chocolate I ate an hour ago. I have a short memory, and I'm easily pleased

Favourite place in the world:
The beach and salt marshes at Hamford Water in Essex. A complete wilderness, only an hour's walk from where I grew up – wonderful!

Want to know more?

Take a look at **nickgifford.co.uk** - find out what's happening in Nick's world, read all about his books and ask Nick your questions.

A HORROR STORY WITH

REAL BITE

Two sharp points of pressure on his neck.

Hard.

Hurting.

The sudden release as his skin broke in two places.

He cried out, but the sound choked off in his throat.

It hurt more than anything he had ever known.

'A contemporary horror story to sink your teeth into'
– *The Times*